BITTERSWEET PROMISES

Montgomery Ink Legacy
Book 1

CARRIE ANN RYAN

BITTERSWEET PROMISES

A MONTGOMERY INK LEGACY NOVEL

By
Carrie Ann Ryan

Bittersweet Promises
A Montgomery Ink Legacy Novel
By: Carrie Ann Ryan
© 2022 Carrie Ann Ryan
eBook ISBN 978-1-950443-83-3
Paperback ISBN 978-1-950443-84-0

Cover Art by Sweet N Spicy Designs

Praise for Carrie Ann Ryan

"Count on Carrie Ann Ryan for emotional, sexy, character driven stories that capture your heart!" – Carly Phillips, NY Times bestselling author

"Carrie Ann Ryan's romances are my newest addiction! The emotion in her books captures me from the very beginning. The hope and healing hold me close until the end. These love stories will simply sweep you away." ~ NYT Bestselling Author Deveny Perry

"Carrie Ann Ryan writes the perfect balance of sweet and heat ensuring every story feeds the soul." - Audrey Carlan, #1 New York Times Bestselling Author

"Carrie Ann Ryan never fails to draw readers in with passion, raw sensuality, and characters that pop off the page. Any book by Carrie Ann is an absolute treat." – New York Times Bestselling Author J. Kenner

"Carrie Ann Ryan knows how to pull your heart-strings and make your pulse pound! Her wonderful Redwood Pack series will draw you in and keep you reading long into the night. I can't wait to see what comes next with the new generation, the Talons. Keep them coming, Carrie Ann!" –Lara Adrian, New York Times bestselling author of CRAVE THE NIGHT

"With snarky humor, sizzling love scenes, and brilliant, imaginative worldbuilding, The Dante's Circle series reads as if Carrie Ann Ryan peeked at my personal wish list!" – NYT Bestselling Author, Larissa Ione

"Carrie Ann Ryan writes sexy shifters in a world full of passionate happily-ever-afters." – *New York Times* Bestselling Author Vivian Arend

"Carrie Ann's books are sexy with characters you can't help but love from page one. They are heat and heart blended to perfection." *New York Times* Bestselling Author Jayne Rylon

Carrie Ann Ryan's books are wickedly funny and deliciously hot, with plenty of twists to keep you guessing. They'll keep you up all night!" USA Today Bestselling Author Cari Quinn

"Once again, Carrie Ann Ryan knocks the Dante's Circle series out of the park. The queen of hot, sexy, enthralling paranormal romance, Carrie Ann is an author not to miss!" *New York Times* bestselling Author Marie Harte

BITTERSWEET PROMISES

New York Times Bestselling Author Carrie Ann Ryan returns with the next generation of Montgomerys and a second chance romance bound in memory and heat.

Leif Montgomery fell hard for Brooke Alder in Paris when they were young, and he thought their fling was just an early taste of what life had in store for him.

But life had other plans, and he didn't find that kind of love—or see Brooke's face—for years.

Until he visits his cousin's house and sees who's moved in next door.

They've both changed: she's a struggling single mom, he's running from a past he's trying to hide while opening up a new tattoo shop. Yet the moment he sees her again, he knows she's the one for him.

And with one look, Brooke knows that she can't

fight the desire that pulled them together before, despite the skeletons in both their closets.

Chapter 1

Leif

"NOT ONLY DID YOU CONVINCE ME TO SOMEHOW GO ON a blind date, it became a double date. How on earth did you work this magic on me, cousin?" I asked Lake as she leaned against the pillar just inside the restaurant.

Lake grinned at me, her dark hair pulled away from her face. She had on this swingy black dress and looked as if she were excited, anxious, nervous, and happy all at the same time. Considering she was bouncing on her toes when usually Lake was calm, cool, and collected, was saying something. "I asked, and you said yes. Because you love me."

"I might love you because we're family, but I still think we're making a mistake." I shook my head and pulled at my shirt sleeves. Lake had somehow convinced me to wear a button-up shirt tucked into gray pants, I even had on shiny shoes. I looked like a damn banker. But if that's what Lake wanted, that's what I would do.

Lake might technically be my cousin, even though we weren't blood-related, but we were more like brother and sister than any of my other cousins.

I had siblings, as did Lake, but with the generational gap, we were at least a decade older than all of our other cousins. That meant, despite the fact that we had lived over an hour apart for most of our lives, we'd grown up more like siblings.

I loved my three younger siblings and talked to them daily. Unlike some blended families, they *were* my brothers and sister and not like strangers or distant family members. I didn't feel a disconnect from the three of them, but Lake was still closer to me.

Probably because we were either heading into our thirties or already there, where most of our other cousins were either just now in their early twenties or still teenagers in high school. With how big we Montgomerys were as a family, it made sense that there would be such a widespread age group. That meant that Lake and I were best friends, cousins, practically siblings, and sometimes the banes of each other's existences.

We were also business owners and partners and saw each other too often these days. That was probably why she convinced me to go on a blind double date. But she had been out with Zach before. I, however, had never met May. Lake had some connection with her that I wasn't sure about, and for some reason Lake's date had said yes to this double date.

And, in the complicated way of family, I had agreed to it. I must have been tired. Or perhaps I'd had too many beers. Because I didn't do blind dates, and recently, I didn't do dates at all.

Lake scanned her phone, then looked up at me, all innocence in her smart gaze. "You shouldn't have told me you wanted to settle down in your old age."

I narrowed my eyes. "I'm still in my early thirties, jerk. Stop calling me old."

"I shouldn't call you old since you're only a few years older than me." She fluttered her eyelashes and I flipped her off, ignoring the stare from the older woman next to me. Though I was a tattoo artist, I didn't have many visible tattoos. Most of mine were on my back and legs, hidden from the world unless I wanted to show them. I hadn't figured out what I wanted on my arms beyond a few small pieces on my wrists and upper shoulders. And since tattoos were permanent, I was taking my time. If a client needed to see my skin with ink to feel comfortable, I'd show them my back. My body was a canvas, so I did what I could to set people at ease.

But I still had the eyebrow piercing and had recently taken out my nose ring. I didn't look too scary for most people. But apparently, flipping off a woman, growling, and cursing a time or two in front of strangers probably made me appear too close to the dark side.

"Yes, I want to settle down, but this will be awkward, won't it? Where the two of us are strangers, and the two of you aren't?" I wanted a life, a future, and yeah, one day to settle down with someone. I just didn't know why I'd mentioned it to Lake in the first place.

"If it helps, May doesn't know Zach, either. So it's a group of strangers, except I know everybody." She clapped her hands together and did her version of an evil laugh, and I just shook my head.

"Considering what you do for a living and how you like to manipulate things in your way, this makes sense. Are you going to be adding a matchmaking company to your conglomerate?"

Lake just fluttered her eyelashes again and laughed. Lake owned a small tech company that made a shit ton of money over the past couple of years. And because she was brilliant at what she did, innovative, and liked pushing money towards women-owned businesses, she owned more than one company at this point and was an investor in mine. I wouldn't be surprised if she found a way to open up a women-owned matchmaking company right here in town.

"It might be fun. I can call it Montgomery Links." Her eyes went wide. "Oh, my God. I have to write that down." She pulled out her phone, began to take notes, and I pinched the bridge of my nose.

"You know I trust you with my actual life, but I don't know if I trust you with my dating life."

Lake tossed her hair behind her shoulder as she continued to type. "Shut up. You love me. And once I finish setting you up, the rest of the family's next."

"Oh, really? You're going to get Daisy and Noah next?" I asked, speaking of two more of our cousins.

"Maybe. Of course, Sebastian's the only one of the younger group that seems to have a serious girlfriend."

I nodded, speaking of our other familial business partner. Sebastian was still a teenager, though in college. He had wanted to open up Montgomery Ink Legacy with me, the full title of our company. There was a legacy to it, and Sebastian had wanted in. So, though he didn't work there full-time, he was putting his future towards us. And in the ways of young love, he and his girlfriend had been together since middle school. The fact that my younger cousin was better at relationships than I was didn't make me feel great. But I was going to ignore that.

"You're not going to start up a matchmaking service, are you? Or maybe an app?"

"Dating apps are ridiculous these days, they practically want you to invest in coins to bid on dates, and that's not something I'm in the mood for. But maybe there's something I can try. I'll add it to my list."

Lake's list of inventions and tech was notorious, and knowing the brilliance of my cousin, she would one day rule the world and might eventually cross everything off that list.

"Oh, here's Zach." Lake's face brightened immediately, and she smiled up at a man with dark hair, piercing gray eyes, and an actual dimple on his cheek.

Tonight was not only about my blind date, but me getting the lay of the land when it came to Zach. I was the first step into meeting the family. Oh, if Zach passed my gauntlet, he would meet the rest of the Montgomerys, and we were mighty. All one hundred of us.

"Zach, you're here." Lake's voice went soft, and she went on her tiptoes even in her high heels as Zach pressed a soft kiss to her lips.

"Of course, I'm here. And you're early, as usual."

Lake blushed and ducked her head. "Well, you know me. I like to be early because being on time is late," she said at the same time I did, mumbling under my breath. It was a familiar refrain when it came to us.

"Zach, good to meet you," I said, holding out my hand.

The other man gripped it firmly and shook. "Nice to meet you too, Leif. I know you might be the one on a blind date soon, but I'm nervous."

I chuckled, shaking my head. "Yeah, I'm pretty nervous too. Though I'm grateful that Lake's trying to look out for me."

My cousin laughed softly. "You totally were not saying that a few minutes ago, but be suave and sophisticated now. Or just be yourself, May's on her way."

I met Zach's gaze and we both rolled our eyes. When I turned toward the door, I saw a woman of average height, with black straight hair, green eyes, and a sweet smile. I didn't know much about May, other than Lake knew her and liked her. If I was going to start dating again after taking time off to get the rest of my life together, I might as well start with someone that one of my best friends liked.

"May, I'm so glad that you're here," Lake said as she hugged the other woman tightly.

As Lake began to bounce on her heels, I realized that my cousin's cool, calm, and collected exterior was only for work. She was bouncing and happy when it came to her friends or when she was nervous. I knew that, of course, but I had forgotten how she had turned into the mogul that she was. It was good to see her relaxed and happy.

Now I just needed to figure out how to do that for myself.

May stood in front of me, and I felt like I was starting middle school all over again. A new school, a new life, and a past that didn't make much sense to anyone else.

I swallowed hard and nodded, not putting out my hand to shake, thinking that would be weird, but I also didn't want to hug her. I didn't even know this woman. Why was everything so awkward? Instead, I lifted my chin. "Hello, May. It's nice to meet you. Lake says only good things."

There, smooth. Not really. Zach began to move out of frame, with Lake at his side as the two went to speak to the hostess, leaving May and me alone.

This wasn't going to be awkward at all.

The woman just smiled at me, her eyes wide. "It's nice to meet you, too. And Lake does speak highly of you. Also, this is very awkward, so I'm so sorry if I say something stupid. I know that your cousin said that I should be set up with you which is great but I'm not great at blind dates and apparently this is a double date and now I'm going to stop talking." She said the words so quickly they all ran into one breath.

I shook my head and laughed. "We're on the same page there."

"Okay, good. It's nice to meet you, Leif Montgomery."

"And it's nice to meet you too, May."

We made our way to Lake and Zach, who had gotten our table, and we all sat down, talking about work and other things. May was in child life development, taught online classes, and was also a nanny.

"I'm actually about to start with a new family soon. I'm excited. I know that being a nanny isn't something that most people strive for, or at least that's what they tell you, but I love being able to work with children and be the person that is there when a single parent or even both parents are out in the workforce, trying to do everything."

I nodded, taking a sip of my beer. "I get you completely. With how my parents worked, I was lucky that they were able to get childcare within the buildings. Since they each owned their own businesses, they made it work. But my family worked long hours, and that's why I ended up being the babysitter a lot of the times when childcare wasn't an option." I cleared my throat. "I'm a lot older than a lot of my cousins," I added.

"Both of us are, but I'm glad that you only said yourself," Lake said, grinning. She leaned into Zach as she spoke, the four of us in a horseshoe-shaped booth. That gave May and me space since this was a first date and still awkward as hell, and so Lake and Zach could cuddle. Not that that was something I needed to be a part of.

"Oh, I'm glad that you didn't judge. The last few dates that I've been on they always gave me weird looks because I think they expected a nanny to be this old crone or someone that's looking for a different job." She shrugged and continued. "When I eventually get married and maybe even start a family, I want to continue my job. I like being there to help another family achieve their goals. And I can't believe I just said start a family on my first date. And that I mentioned that I've been on a few other dates." She let out a breath. "I'm notoriously bad at dating. Like, the worst. Just warning you."

I laughed, shaking my head. "I'm rusty at it, so don't worry." And even though I said that, I had a feeling that May felt no spark towards me, and I didn't feel anything towards her. She was nice and pleasant, and I could probably consider her a friend one day. But there wasn't any spark. May's eyes weren't dancing. She wasn't leaning forward, trying to touch my hand across the table. We were just sitting there casually, enjoying a really good steak, as Lake and Zach enjoyed their date.

By the end of dinner, I didn't want dessert, and neither did May, so we said goodbye to the other couple, who decided to stay. I walked May to her car, ignoring Lake's warning look, but I didn't know what exactly she was warning me about.

"Thanks for dinner," May said. "I could have paid.

I know this is a blind date and all that, but you didn't have to pay."

I shook my head. "I paid for the four of us because I wanted to be nice. I'll make Lake pay next time."

May beamed. "Yes, I like that. You guys are a good family."

"Anyway," I said, clearing my throat as I stuck my hands in my pockets. "I guess I'll see you around."

May just looked at me, threw her head back, and laughed. "You're right. You are rusty at this."

"Sorry." Heat flushed my skin, and I resisted the urge to tug on my eyebrow ring.

"It's okay. No spark. I'm used to it. I don't spark well."

"May, I'm sorry." I cringed. "It's not you."

"Oh, God, please don't say that. 'It's not you. It's me. You're working on yourself. You're just so busy with work.' I've heard it all."

"Seriously?" I asked. May was hot. Nice, but there just wasn't a spark.

She shrugged. "It's okay. I'll probably see you around sometime because I am friends with Lake. However, I am perfectly fine having this be our one and only. You'll find your person. It's okay that it's not me." And with that, she got in the car and left, leaving me standing there.

Well then. Tonight wasn't horrible, but it wasn't great. I got in my car, and instead of heading home where I'd be alone, watching something on some streaming service while I drank a beer and pretended that I knew what I was doing with my life, I headed into Montgomery Ink Legacy.

We were the third branch of the company and the first owned by our generation. Montgomery Ink was the tattoo shop in downtown Denver. While there were open spots for some walk-ins and special circumstances, my father, aunt, and their team had years' worth of waiting lists. They worked their asses off and made sure to get in everybody that they could, but people wanted Austin Montgomery's art. Same with my aunt, Maya.

There was another tattoo shop down in Colorado Springs, owned by my parents' cousins, who I just called aunt and uncle because we were close enough that using real titles for everybody got confusing. Montgomery Ink Too was thriving down there, and they had waiting lists as well. My family could have opened more shops and gone nationwide, even global if they wanted to, but they liked keeping it how it was, in the family and those connected.

We were a branch, but our own in the making. I had gone into business with Lake, of course, and Sebastian, when he was ready, as well as Nick. Nick was my best friend. I had known him for ages, and he had wanted to be part of something as well. He might not be a Montgomery by name, but he had eaten over at my family's house enough times throughout the years that he was practically a Montgomery. And he had invested in the company as well, and so now we were nearly a year into owning the shop and trying not to fail.

I pulled into the parking lot, grateful it was still open since we didn't close until nine most nights, and greeted Nick, who was still working.

Sebastian was in the back, going over sketches with a client, and I nodded at him. He might be eighteen, but he was still in training, an apprentice, and was working his ass off to learn.

"Date sucked then?" Sebastian asked, and Nick just rolled his eyes and went back to work on a client's wrist.

"I don't want to talk about it," I groaned.

The rest of the staff was off since Nick would close up on his own. Sebastian was just there since he didn't have homework or a date with Marley.

"Was she hot at least?" Sebastian asked, and the client, a woman in her sixties, bopped him on the head with her bag gently.

"Sebastian Montgomery. Be nice."

Sebastian blushed. "Sorry, Mrs. Anderson."

I looked over at the woman and grinned. "Hi, Mrs. Anderson. It's nice to see you out of the classroom."

She narrowed her eyes at me, even though they filled with laughter. "I needed my next Jane Austen tattoo, thank you very much," the older woman said as she went back to working with Sebastian. She had been my and then Sebastian's English teacher. The fact that she was on her fifth tattoo with some literary quote told me that I had been damn lucky in most of my teachers growing up.

She was kick-ass, and I had a feeling that she would let Sebastian do the tattoo for her rather than just have him work on the design with me as we did for most of the people who came in. He had learned under my father and was working under me now. It was strange to think that he wasn't a little kid anymore. But he was in a long-term relationship, kicking ass in college, and knew what he wanted to do with his life.

I might know what I want to do with my work life, but everything else seemed a little off.

"So it didn't work out?" Nick asked as he walked up to the front desk with the clients after going over aftercare.

"Not really," I said, looking down at my phone.

The client, a woman in her mid-twenties with bright pink hair, a lip ring, and kind eyes, leaned over the desk to look at me.

"You'll find someone, Leif. Don't worry."

I looked at our regular and shook my head. "Thanks, Kim. Too bad that you don't swing this way."

I winked as I said it, a familiar refrain from both of us.

Kim was married to a woman named Sonya, and the two of them were happy and working on in vitro with donated sperm for their first kid.

"Hey, I'm sorry too that I'm a lesbian. I'll never know what it means to have Leif Montgomery. Or any Montgomery, since I found my love far too quickly. I mean, what am I ever going to do not knowing the love of a Montgomery?"

Mrs. Anderson chuckled from her chair, Sebastian held back a snort, and I just looked at Nick, who rolled his eyes and helped Kim out of the place.

I was tired, but it was okay. The date wasn't all bad. May was nice. But it felt like I didn't have much right then.

And then Nick sat in front of me, scowled, and I realized that I did have something. I had my friends and my family. I didn't need much more.

"So, you and May didn't work out?"

I raised a brow. "You knew her name? Did I tell you that?"

Nick shook his head. "Lake did."

That made sense, considering the two of them spoke as much as we did. "So, was it your idea to set me up on a blind date?"

"Fuck no. That was all Lake. I just do what she says. Like we all do."

I sighed and went through my appointments for the next day. "We're busy for the next month. That's good, right?" I asked.

"You're the business genius here. I just play with ink. But yes, that's good. Now, don't let your cousin set you up any more dates. Find them for yourself. You know what you're doing."

"So says the man who dates less than me."

"That's what you think. I'm more private about it. As it should be." I flipped him off as he stood up, then he gestured towards a stack of bills in the corner. "You have a few personal things that made their way here. Don't want you to miss out on them before you head home."

"Thanks, bro."

"No problem. I'm going to help Sebastian with his consult, and then I'll clean up. You should head home. Though you're doing it alone, so I feel sorry for you."

"Fuck you," I called out.

"Fuck you, too."

"Boys," Mrs. Anderson said, in that familiar English teacher refrain, and both Nick and I cringed before saying, "Sorry," simultaneously.

Sebastian snickered, then went back to work, and I headed towards the edge of the counter, picking up the stack of papers. Most were bills, some were random papers that needed to be filed or looked over. Some were just junk mail. But there was one letter, written in block print that didn't look familiar. Chills went up my spine and I opened it, wondering what the fuck this was. Maybe it was someone asking to buy my house. I got a lot of handwritten letters for that, but I didn't think this was going to be that. I swallowed hard, slid open the paper, and froze.

"I'll find you, boy. Oops. Looks like I already did. Be waiting. I know you miss me."

I let the paper hit the top of the counter and swallowed hard, trying to remain cool so I didn't worry anyone else.

I didn't know exactly who that was from, but I had a horrible feeling that they wouldn't wait long to tell me.

Chapter 2

Brooke

"MOMMY. I THINK I'M SICK."

At those words that every mother dreaded hearing, I looked into the rearview mirror, trying to simultaneously keep one eye on the road, as Luke leaned out of the car seat that he was nearly too big for—he was nearly ready for the booster seat—but my little boy who wasn't so little anymore was currently clutching his stomach like he was ready to throw up.

"Do you need me to pull over, buddy?" I asked, hoping I didn't have to do so right now. I needed to beat the movers to the house. Thanks to a quirk of fate, a bad connection, a storm, a flood, and a water main break, I was two days late getting to our new home.

I had wanted to get everything set up for the movers. Instead, I was going to barely beat them to the house. Thankfully, my realtor was a godsend and had gotten everything ready for me, but I felt like I was behind.

I always felt like I was behind these days.

"I'm just nervous, Mommy."

I held back my look of relief at those words and swallowed hard. I knew he'd gotten the saying from me, but it sounded adorable coming out of his mouth.

"I'm nervous too, Luke. But this is exciting. A brand-new yard. A big boy's bed."

As long as the bed showed up from the furniture store the next day. Tonight we would be roughing it with sleeping bags that were currently stuffed in the back of my SUV.

"But what if I don't like school? What if school is hard?"

"Then I'm here to help you. You know I love school."

"Because you're a pro-fes-sor." He mumbled the word, sounding it out, and I was proud that he at least got that far with it. Usually, he couldn't say the word that well. But my baby boy was getting older and he was losing that little boy voice of his.

"I *am* going to be a professor. Are you excited to meet the neighbors? And your new schoolmates?"

"I just want them to like me. Because I like you, Mommy."

My heart warmed, and I wanted to reach back and grip his hand and tell him everything would be okay. Only I wasn't sure that it was because we were picking up our lives and changing everything.

I had to tell myself I could do this. I had been a single mom for my baby boy's entire existence. We were a team, a duo. We could work with anything. Face anything. Except for maybe a cross-country move with just the two of us in my SUV to a place that I hadn't lived in years.

But California and Europe were behind me. And now it was time for a whole new adventure with the love of my life.

"Does your stomach feel okay?" I asked, hoping it was just nerves and he wasn't going to throw up in the back of my car during the last few miles of the drive. We had driven all the way from California to Colorado. It hadn't been easy, and my head ached, but there was no way I could have flown with Luke and the stuff we needed. It was easier to do the drive as a team, rather than hoping my car would get to where I wanted.

"I feel better. Thank you, Mommy."

I held back a sigh of relief as I pulled into the

neighborhood, looking around at the large trees, green grass, and blue skies. I loved it here in Colorado, though it had been a while since I lived here. But I did love Arvada. I had grown up in Westminster, which was only about five minutes north. The suburbs of Colorado were all tangled together, and while I lived in one burb, I was going to work in a burb about two suburbs down. It made sense to anyone who lived here, and I knew that this was the right decision. Though my family wasn't here anymore, and losing them had hurt me beyond measure, my sense of home was here. I knew this area and its roads like the back of my hand. Even with the new neighborhoods, the new businesses, and constant changes, everything still felt the same.

That's why I was coming home. That, and a job offer I couldn't refuse. So now my California baby was going to become a Colorado Rockie. And I could not wait to see how much he loved it.

His gaze had been on the mountains for most of the trip, his eyes wide as he went on and on about wanting to see bears and mountain lions and anything with park rangers. I just had to hope that none of those, including the ranger, ended up on our doorstep. Maybe when we visited the mountains, and the forest, I wouldn't mind seeing a bear.

From far, *far* away.

The neighborhood was a few years old, one of the newer developments built after I had moved to France and then California. It had been more than six years since I had lived here, after all, things were going to change rapidly. And yet things still felt the same. The roads had the same names, the people were still friendly, and the skies were still blue. That is, until the skies were no longer blue and bright, and four different seasons all happened in one day. But that was something I was used to. And that was home.

These houses were decently sized, with large yards, but not so big that you didn't get to know your neighbor or spend every weekend doing yard work until you fainted.

It was going to be a good place for me to meet other single moms and families. That way Luke wasn't lonely, and we weren't living in a far too expensive apartment while trying to do everything at once.

Our home was at the end of a cul-de-sac, surrounded by the old trees they built around and the younger saplings they planted after they finished.

I loved the look of it, the two-story home having called to me from the online listing. I had come out to see the place in person, as well as at least twenty others during my quick weekend out here. This was the place I had loved, and thankfully the previous owners had taken my offer.

The owners had loved the place, had worked with the builders personally to make it theirs, but were moving thanks to their jobs. I didn't know much about the Montgomery Builders, or Montgomery Inc., as they were called, but my realtor said that they were the best in the business. That meant the house was sturdy and nice. That was fine with me. As long as there was a place for Luke, I was happy.

We pulled in and I sighed dreamily as I looked at the place, and in relief about the fact that we had actually beaten the movers.

"We're home, Luke. What do you think?"

Luke strained in his seat and looked around. "It's beauty-ful, Mom. Is it ours?"

I sighed softly and looked back at him. "It's ours. Pretty nifty, isn't it?"

"I like nifty."

I grinned and got out of the car quickly, having pulled off to the farthest edge of the driveway so the movers could back in easily, and went to get Luke out of his seat. He had already unbuckled himself—the kid's far too smart for his own good—and I helped him out of the car before I took his hand and we looked up at our new home.

"Well, what do you think?" I asked. Luke hadn't been with me when I picked the house, though he had seen pictures and had done the online tour with me countless times.

"I love my room." He grinned up at me, and I just smiled. I knew that this was a huge change for us, but it was the only decision I could have made. Therefore, it had to be the best one.

"Okay, let's get ready for the movers."

I clapped my hands, pulled out the key that the realtor had given me that morning when I stopped by the office quickly to sign the rest of the papers, and headed into the house.

I smiled softly as I looked at the giant basket on the counter, courtesy of my realtor, a woman that I had quickly become friends with. She was a grandmother, worked her butt off, and loved what she did.

Inside the basket was food, goodies, and a present for Luke. My eyes filled with tears, and I looked around and noticed a few other welcome home gifts, including a plant that I would probably kill, but I would do my best to keep alive.

"Mommy, we have presents?"

"We do, Luke. They're welcoming us home."

His eyes went wide, confused as he looked around the open and empty space. "Home?"

My heart did that little clutch thing, wondering once again if I was ruining my son's life. I swore moms everywhere throughout history all had lists in their minds of ways that they were ruining their children's lives.

"We'll make it home. What do you say? Want to be my partner?"

"Okay!" he said, clapping his hands.

"Knock, knock," a stranger's unfamiliar voice said from the doorway. I whirled, pulling Luke behind me, my pulse racing.

A woman stood there, her dark hair flowing around her face. She had on a white blouse, comfortable gray pants, and smiled wide.

"Hello?" I said, my voice cool.

I didn't know this woman, but if she was a neighbor or something, I should probably not be a jerk and threaten her for scaring the crap out of me.

The woman's eyes widened and she held up both hands. "I'm so sorry. I did not mean to scare you. I'm your neighbor, Lake. Lake Montgomery. I saw you pull in and the door was open. I just wanted to make sure everything was okay and welcome you." She bent down and picked up a casserole dish and a bag. "Your realtor, Nancy, said that you would be here and that I should welcome you if I was home. And since I'm working from my home office today, I figured I would. I swear I didn't mean to startle you."

I let out a breath, vaguely remembering that my realtor had mentioned Lake. She lived alone next door, and her family was somehow connected to the company that built the house.

"Hi. Sorry. You did startle me, but it's been a long trip."

Luke stuck his head out from behind my legs and

pulled on my jeans. "Hi. I'm Luke. Mom says not to talk to strangers, are you a stranger?"

I closed my eyes and laughed. "Hello, I am Brooke. This is my son, Luke."

Lake grinned, her hands full. "Hello, Luke and Brooke. I'm your neighbor, and I finished all my work today, so if you need help lifting anything heavy, I'm here."

I smiled, wondering if this was a sign that moving here was the right choice. "Speaking of lifting, let me help you with whatever you're holding now. And thank you. Seriously. Though you do *not* have to help with the movers."

"Oh right. Sorry." Lake laughed, her whole face brightening. "I baked a casserole. It's mostly the dreaded vegetables," she said, eyeing Luke, who just grinned.

"I like vegetables."

Lake's eyes widened. "I'm going to have to tell my mother that people actually do like vegetables. I'm shocked."

I shook my head, laughing even through the mental gymnastics of the day. "He loves his veggies, and I count it as a blessing."

Luke proudly puffed his chest. "Broccoli's the best. And brussels sprouts."

Lake nearly dropped her packages and I laughed, taking the dish from her hands.

"I know. I know. I think Luke likes the way I cook them. I roast them," I added.

Lake smiled. "I do, too, but I feel like I need to do better. Anyway, I'm off for the day, and I just need to change clothes, but I can help you. Nancy said that your movers were coming through a bunch of delays, so you have me if you need me."

I blinked at the generosity once again. "You don't have to do that. We can handle it."

"We're a team," Luke said, and I grinned down at him, ruffling his hair.

"We are a team."

"The best team ever," Lake said, grinning. "I seriously don't mind helping. The people that used to live here helped as well, although my siblings, parents, and cousins were all here to help, too. There's a lot of us."

"You said you're a Montgomery?" I asked, slowly piecing together what she'd said before. I needed some caffeine soon if I was going to be able to function the rest of the day.

"I am. You'll probably meet more of us, because a few of us do live in the neighborhood."

"I met a Montgomery from Colorado once, when I was in Paris." I hadn't meant to say that. I had no idea why I had. It wasn't like I'd thought about him.

Much.

Or at all.

Or ever.

Why had I brought it up in the first place?

Lake's eyes widened. "Really? Well, it's probably not us since it is a common name, but if you meet one in Colorado, they're more than likely to be related to me. In fact, my cousin is on his way to bum food off of me since it's my turn to feed him, so I can probably borrow his muscles to help you out, too."

"You feed him often?" I asked.

Lake nodded her head. "Yeah, we're more like siblings, and we take turns feeding each other so we're not constantly cooking for one."

"Oh, I guess that makes sense."

"We try. Anyway, do you need help?"

As soon as she asked the words again, a large truck pulled in in front of my house. My eyes widened, I looked out at my still full SUV, my kid bouncing on his toes, and sighed, giving in. "Okay. I could really use your help."

"Welcome to Colorado."

"Thank you. Now I just have to not panic when I think about everything I have to do."

"It's okay, Mom. We're a team. Lake too."

Lake just beamed. "Exactly. Let me go change. Oh, there's my cousin now. I'll tell him we're roping him in."

"You don't have to do that. He does not have to help." I already felt bad about this near stranger helping me out like this.

"Yes, he does. He's a Montgomery. It's what we do."

A man in a large gray truck got out, and I did my best not to look too hard at his jeans. At the way that he filled them out, the way that he moved, at the fact that he was very ripped.

I shook myself out of it. I might have dated a few times in the past five years, but it had been long enough for me to apparently lose my mind.

Then he moved forward and turned, and I nearly fell right off of my front step.

Lake was talking to him, but I knew that face, those eyes, those cheekbones. That jaw.

I knew those lips, those hands. I knew everything.

From when I was eighteen, in a country not my own, in a memory that didn't even feel like mine anymore.

"Ms. Adler?" a man with a gruff voice asked, and I looked towards the man in charge of the moving truck and smiled.

"That's me. We're here." The whirring in my brain got louder, and I swallowed hard, my throat suddenly dry.

"You just tell us where to unload, and we've got you. I'll get the few forms for you, but we know the drill."

"And she's got helpers," Lake added as she moved

forward, the man who wasn't a stranger but apparently her cousin at her side.

I turned to them, eyes wide, as Leif Montgomery tripped and nearly fell, staring at me.

"*You*. Brooke?" he asked.

Lake looked between us, her eyes wide, and I gripped Luke's hand, looked at the mover, then back at Leif.

A blast from the past.

And apparently, the Montgomery I had met in Paris.

Chapter 3

Leif

I STARED AT BROOKE, WONDERING IF I WAS SEEING things. I remembered that long reddish-brown hair of hers. Those hazel eyes had always captured me. She was a little below average in height. That was always a fun play against my six-foot-four frame. She was also all curves in the right places and had only grown sexier in the time we'd been apart.

Was she truly here? This blast from the past?

I let out another breath and helped move the last box into the house, doing my best to keep my eyes off the woman that had haunted my dreams for far too long.

She held the clipboard, a pen in her hair, another in her hands, a third pen attached to the cleavage on her top.

I was doing my best not to think about that particular one.

She was organized, meticulous, and had been the fantasy of my dreams for too long.

"You're staring."

I looked over at my cousin and shook my head. "I'm just in awe over here. It's spooky. I don't understand."

Lake snorted at my attempt to not sound like I'd been drooling in my own memories. "I'm the one who has questions, Leif. Not you."

"I suppose that's all right. Is she seriously your neighbor now?" I kept my voice low since Brooke was walking in, still staring at the clipboard, and I didn't want her to think I was talking about her.

Even though, *of course*, I was talking about her.

The woman I'd shared a hot and steamy couple of weeks in Paris with was now living next to my cousin. The cousin who happened to be one of my best friends.

In all the places, in all the world, she had to show up here.

After all these years, after so many unending questions because I didn't have her anymore.

She had just shown up.

I pushed those thoughts to the back of my mind and looked down at the kid who was staring up at me. I could feel his gaze boring into my side, so I tried not to act like a growly asshole.

"Hey, Luke, is it?" I asked

"That's me. Luke. Why are you so big? And why do you have something on your face?"

I held back a laugh. "I'm big because I'm a grown-up and most of the guys in my family are all this tall. I have a beard. My dad has an even *bigger* beard."

I knelt in front of him, my shoulders aching from the unexpected moving day. I'd spent the entire morning working on a client's back, bent over to get the perfect angle, so my client was comfortable. It meant that I was the one with back pain at the end of the day. One of my friends wore corsets these days to help with his stature, and I thought maybe I should try. Maybe I would force Nick to do it with me, so I wasn't alone.

I was sure my dad had even done it once before, but my dad's torso was so long that he would probably have had it custom-made.

Either way, though, I was tired and a little out of my element.

I knew kids, and one day I wanted kids of my own. I was the oldest cousin by more than a few years. Hell, I had been a grown adult when my parents adopted my two younger siblings. I had been packing for my college visit when the call came through that my parents would be parents again.

I knew how to act around kids. And although none of my generation had started the next generation yet, I knew we would soon. I helped raise my siblings and cousins, and had been their designated babysitter for years. Hell, I still was sometimes.

And yet, why did I feel so awkward around this boy?

He was cute for sure. He looked just like his mom, with dark red hair and light eyes.

A mom that I hadn't seen in years. Due to the timing, I knew this kid wasn't mine, so it wasn't like a secret baby situation, but I had still done the math just in case. It had been a shock to see Brooke standing there, her eyes wide, looking glorious and gorgeous as ever.

And here I was, kneeling in front of her son, wondering who the hell his father was and why it looked like she was here alone.

Not that I was going to do anything about it.

I couldn't do anything about it.

I was going on a dating moratorium, at least that's what I told myself. The date with May had been okay, but the lack of sparks had killed my desire to try to date again.

Especially with a woman that clearly hadn't wanted

me before, no matter how hot our time together had been in Paris.

And she had enough baggage that she wasn't going to be looking at me and wanting more. I wasn't even sure why I was thinking about it.

I was just the big, bearded, tattoo artist, art-school dropout in other people's eyes. It didn't matter that the word artist was in the name. Most people didn't think of me as such.

I was fine with that. My friends and family were, too. But many of the women I had dated hadn't been.

I didn't even know what Brooke would think, but that wouldn't matter.

I was just the stranger with the beard that this kid looked curious about.

As if he had never seen a roughneck like me.

"Can I feel your beard?" Luke asked, and I shrugged.

"I guess it's okay. If it's okay with your mom." I looked up as Brooke looked down at us, something in her eyes I couldn't quite read.

She smiled and slid her hand over her son's head. "Of course, you can. If it's okay with Mr. Montgomery."

I raised a brow, wondering if I liked being called Mr. Montgomery out of a mouth that had once been wrapped around my cock. Maybe I did.

"There's a lot of Montgomerys around here, Brooke. Maybe he should call me Leif."

She cringed and I wondered what that was about.

"I guess you're right. Although, it's kind of odd if there are so many Montgomerys, I run into you here."

There was a deafening silence, and she cleared her throat while I just stared at her, wanting answers, wanting more. Knowing I couldn't have it. Again.

"Sure, Luke, honey. You can feel his beard. Just be gentle, please, and don't pull."

That reminded me of the time she had pulled because she had been tugging me closer to her pussy.

That was enough of that.

"Okay." Luke patted my beard and smiled. I lowered my head slightly, so he didn't have to reach as much. "It's soft."

"I use beard oil. It's always good to have good beard care." I winked at him, and he giggled.

"Will I have a beard?" Luke asked, his eyes wide and curious.

"When you're older, sure. I don't see why not." I looked up at Brooke again, ignoring the tightening in my gut. "What do you think? Will the kid look good with the beard?"

Brooke looked at me, blinked, and smiled. "I think you would look quite dashing with a beard, Luke. But you still have a few years to go. Remember, you are not supposed to grow up too quickly. You need to give Mommy some time to get accustomed."

"What's acc-ustomed-ed?" Luke asked, sounding out the word.

"Accustomed. Getting used to it. So you have to give your mom time before you grow up and get a huge beard." I roughed up his hair slightly and he grinned at me, smiling his mom's smile.

"I can wait. I think it will be a while until I am as big as you. But Mom's not big. Maybe I'll be like her."

"I think your mom is just the right size," I said without thinking. When I clamped my mouth shut, I stood up, stretching my back. "So, what do you think? Does everything look good? Did you empty the truck?" I asked, trying not to act as if this was awkward.

Brooke let out a soft breath. "Yes. Thank you. You honestly did not have to do all of this. I am forever grateful."

"We are always here to help," Lake put in. She had been mysteriously silent for the entire conversation, and I knew she would have questions. Of course, the other woman would have questions. If I weren't careful, she would bring those questions to the rest of the family, and then they would be a cacophony of Montgomery intrusiveness.

I loved my family. I honestly did. I loved how we were always there for each other. Only sometimes, it was almost a little bit too much. Because yes, we could keep secrets, of course we could keep secrets, yet we all wanted to help one another so much sometimes that it felt almost overwhelming.

Sometimes, despite myself, I had to remind my own mind that I was a Montgomery as well. Even after over twenty years of being immersed in this family, growing up with it and remembering that I hadn't been born into it. Maybe by blood, but not by situation.

"Seriously though, you guys have no idea how much it helped." Brooke put her hand around Luke's shoulders as the kid leaned into his mom.

It was so strange to see Brooke as a mom. She was good at it from what I could tell in the little amount of time I'd seen her at it. She had kept one eye on what she was doing, one eye on making sure that Lake and I and the movers knew where to put things, and a random third eye that must only exist for parents on her kid the whole time. Luke had been safe and secure and had snacks when he needed them.

She was a wizard, just like my mom was.

It was still just so odd to see Brooke in that situation.

"You're Lake's new neighbor. We were not going to let you do it by yourself." I nearly growled the words, and I ignored the pointed look from my cousin.

Brooke just blinked at me and shrugged. "With the timing, we ran late, and the movers were early, so I'm glad it all worked out. I would've been able to do it myself, as I did when I moved to California, but I am truly grateful. And now my house is full of boxes, and I only know for sure where my son's sheets are for his bed, but that's about it. I would offer to cook you dinner or something to say thank you, but I don't think that will happen since I don't know where my pans are. Maybe another time."

She was looking at Lake as she spoke, not looking at me at all. I had to wonder if that was on purpose. I had seen anger and surprise in her gaze when I had pulled up, but why would there be anger on her part?

She was the one who had left. Yes, because her trip had been over, but she hadn't shown up when we planned to meet.

She had decided no.

So it wasn't my fault.

But laying blame wasn't going to help this current predicament.

My cousin smiled. "Oh, you're not going to cook for us. That casserole that I brought over is for you tomorrow. That way, you don't have to cook tomorrow, either. However, I have something in the crockpot over at my house that I have been watching with the camera I have on in my kitchen, so you guys will come over and eat." Lake nodded quickly as if she were ordering soldiers and she was the general.

Brooke blinked as she stared at Lake. "You seriously don't need to do that. I just met you. You're kind, I swear. But we can order in, or indeed have that casserole."

"Think nothing of it. Let me make you a home-cooked meal and thank you for letting me help organize. You have no idea how much that helps me." My cousin winked, then stared at me as if willing me to say something.

I shrugged. "She's not lying. If she could organize the world, she would. I think she gets it from my aunt."

"Your aunt, as in her mom?" Brooke asked, looking between the two of us.

Lake and I looked at each other and laughed. "No, technically, Lake is the daughter of my father's cousin."

"I have no idea what that means," Brooke said, her voice dry. "So, you guys are like, second cousins, or first cousins once removed?"

"These are questions we do not ask," Lake said solemnly, though her eyes danced.

"Exactly. All of us in this generation are just cousins. Getting too technical hurts our heads, and we were raised practically as siblings, so it doesn't matter. But my aunt, and hers, since that's what we call her, is into planners and organizing. Lake is just like her. And is, indeed, taking over the world with her business."

"What do you do?" Luke asked, dancing on his toes.

"You see? These are things we should discuss over dinner. You can relax. And then you can sleep in your own home and get on with the rest of your lives, knowing that you have a busybody neighbor next door who is always willing to help." Lake beamed, and I just laughed, knowing that there was no way that Brooke and Luke were getting out of this.

Lake wanted to help, and frankly, I figured she wanted a friend. And I wanted answers.

"Plus, you know, we're not technically strangers. And I'm not just talking about all of the sweat and tears thrown out today. It seems you know my cousin." Lake winked at Brooke, and I cursed under my breath, trying not to be too loud since Luke was standing right next to me.

Brooke pressed her lips together while pointedly not looking at me. "Oh. Well, that was a long time ago."

"What was a long time ago, Mommy?" Luke asked, his voice curious.

There was nothing but curiosity in how Lake was looking at me as if she needed answers, and Brooke was glaring daggers at the both of us.

"Dinner sounds lovely. I guess it would be nice to catch up," Brooke said, her voice clipped.

What had I done all those years ago? Did she hate me? I sure as hell hoped not. I wasn't sure what else I was supposed to do. And fuck yes, I was going to catch up on something we should've done nearly ten years ago.

We left Brooke and Luke to make up their sleeping bags and have some alone time as I followed Lake over to her house.

Her place smelled like pulled pork and I groaned.

"Did you make the brioche rolls?" I asked, my mouth watering.

"Of course, I did. And coleslaw and baked beans. I should make a salad or something. Don't kids need vegetables?"

I just shook my head. "I think coleslaw is a vegetable."

"It's covered in sauce. I don't think that counts. You would think I would know that since we have so many kids in the family."

"This feels new, doesn't it?" I asked, feeling odd. I leaned against the counter, wondering if I should have a beer. Should I drink in front of the kid? It just reminded me that I didn't know this Brooke. I knew the eighteen-year-old Brooke, back in the day when we had been kids. Both of us had learned that wine was delicious and available in Paris.

We weren't those kids anymore, and now she was a mom, seemingly living out here on her own, and I felt like I was running in place.

"Are you going to tell me what happened?"

I shook my head. "What do you mean?"

"You know exactly what I mean, Leif. You guys knew each other. From when?"

"From a long time ago, Lake."

She cleared her throat and bit her lip. "Luke isn't yours, is he?"

I blinked at her before I scoffed. "You know exactly how I came into this family, Lake. How my birth mom hid me from my dad, and I showed up when Mom was gone, and I had no one else. Dad didn't even know I existed. He didn't ignore me, didn't push me away, didn't abandon me. I lost time with him because I didn't know who he was. Do you think I would do that to another kid? Do you think I would act the way that I did just then, trying to be as casual as fuck when it comes to her, if I thought for a second that was my kid? Jesus Christ, Lake. You know me better than that."

Lake blushed. "I'm sorry. It was just the first thing that popped into my mind when a single mom shows up at the house, and you guys look like you know each other. That was wrong of me. I didn't think that all the way through." Lake moved forward, hugged me tight. "I'm sorry."

She stepped away and went to get a bottle of wine out of the fridge, as well as the sparkling juice.

"It's okay. I did the math myself. It's been over ten years, though. Luke isn't mine."

"Wait, that means you knew her in what, Paris? Oh

my God. The *Paris* girl?" Her voice got high-pitched and I saw hope in her eyes.

"Yes, it's the Paris girl. That also means she's the girl who never showed up when she was supposed to. The girl that chose another life over wanting anything more with me. That's *that* Brooke. But don't worry, things won't be weird."

"Well, that's a lie."

"What do you mean?" I asked, even though I knew what she meant.

"Because things are already weird. You should talk to her."

I took the glass of wine she handed me and shook my head. "Yes, I'm totally going to ask her why she didn't show up when she was supposed to. Why we never made a go of things, especially when she's exhausted after moving and possibly driving for who knows how many days to get here? I don't even know the whole story because I don't know her. But yes, I should totally ask these questions when she's in front of her kid and my cousin. Makes total sense."

Lake blinked slowly. "You know, I feel like you're getting more sarcastic in your old age."

"I'm not old. Watch your tone," I teased.

"Is that a gray hair in your beard? I bet you that's why the kid was so in awe of it. Because it's gray."

I scowled then froze as the doorbell rang.

"There they are. Are you ready for this?" she asked.

"I'm going to go with no. Let's do it."

Lake gave me a weird look and set her glass down. "I don't want you to get hurt, Leif. You're my best friend."

"I'm fine," I lied. "It's just a girl from the past. A girl, from the looks of it, who needs help. She said she was a single mom? Maybe she doesn't have a support system. Especially if we are the only ones that showed up to help her today, we can be her friends. I'll get over whatever the hell's going on in my mind. I promise. I always do."

"Maybe that's the problem, Leif. You're good at getting over it. I'm quite sure you know what that means."

My cousin kissed me on the cheek and then went to answer the door, Luke's laughter filling the house faster than anything I thought possible.

And I stood there, wondering if I was making a mistake. If I should just go.

But as I looked at Brooke and her wide eyes, I knew I couldn't go.

I couldn't before. I wasn't going to do it now.

Chapter 4

Brooke

I LOVED DENVER. IT HAD BEEN YEARS SINCE I HAD lived anywhere near the city, the mountains, the atmosphere. Yet it felt as if I had come home.

Though I had been to more than my fair share of cities, Denver always felt different to me. I could easily find my way around the city as if it had always been ingrained in my mind.

Part of me might have found that weird, but since I used to love travel, figuring out the lay of the land was usually the first thing that I did.

My home in Arvada was just now feeling comfortable, and I was as unpacked as I was going to be for a while. Today I was planning to explore the downtown area a little bit more. I would be working at the university in another suburb, so I wouldn't be in the downtown area often. But I used to like coming here for lunch, coffee, or to enjoy myself.

I loved that I could get the "city feel" and look at the Rocky Mountains all at the same time.

Luke was at kindergarten, that odd feeling of my baby growing up twisting the knife in my heart a little bit deeper. He had been in daycare and PreK since he was a baby, since I was a single mom and I needed to work, and my boy loved being with others. He loved socializing and learning and was just a joy to be around most days.

At least that's what his teachers told me.

But today was his first day of half-day kindergarten, and I was nervous.

Parents weren't allowed to stay and watch since that wasn't our job. And I needed to get used to this because even though we were in a new city and a new environment, this should be easy for him.

He had held my hand as we walked into the building and then had run off to his teacher, waving behind him after he said goodbye to me.

That knife dug a little deeper, and I told myself that this was good.

I told myself that though Luke and I were a team, it was good that he was so independent. That he was ready to face his new day and fears and was ready to leave me behind.

Alone. Because he didn't need his mommy.

I nearly kicked myself at that thought, knowing I was being overdramatic. Just because Luke could handle things on his own for a few minutes didn't mean he didn't need me.

And I was going to be working full-time, long hours, and starting a new phase of my career soon. I should be grateful that he could be so independent.

That afternoon, his new nanny and I would go and pick him up.

I had interviewed May before I moved here. We'd done online chats, and I had met with her when I came to buy the house. I liked May and figured that she and Luke would be a good team when I wasn't around.

I wasn't one of those mothers who felt that Luke gaining a relationship with his nanny or caretaker would take anything away from our relationship. I didn't believe that that could happen. Because Luke and I *were* a team, and he needed other members on that team to be a self-reliant and healthy human being.

So, this afternoon, Luke would spend the day with May, and I would head to work for a couple of meetings. This morning was all about breathing in that mountain and city air that somehow meshed well into an amalgamation that was an Denver.

There was just one street that I absolutely loved. It seemed to have nearly everything that I needed, and none of it was cookie-cutter or franchise. And every single one of my favorite places was still there.

There was a little boutique called Eden where I had bought my first pair of fancy shoes. I would probably go shopping there again as long as the merchandise felt about the same. As I walked around the tables and decorations, I smiled, knowing that I would still come back here though I was on a budget.

The woman who owned the place was gorgeous, with long, nearly auburn hair, and though it had been nearly a decade, she still looked the same to me.

"Hello there, is there anything I can do for you?"

I shook my head as I smiled at the owner. "I'm just walking around browsing today. It's been a while since I've been here. I was pleased to see that you guys are still here."

The owner grinned. "I'm glad that I'm here, too. We had a few facelifts and updates along the way since we first opened all those years ago, but I'm proud to say that Eden isn't going anywhere anytime soon."

"That's good to know. And, I'm looking at that scarf over there, I think I have to have it."

"My name is Sierra, by the way. It's nice to meet you."

"Brooke. Thank you for being so welcoming."

"I'm just glad that you're back. No matter the time between, repeat customers always make me happy."

We spoke for a little bit longer as we went over the scarf, the silk smooth on my hands.

"I love it. And I think this will be my welcome home present to me."

"So, you're moving to the area? I think that's what I got from what you were saying."

We went over to the cash register as Sierra packaged up my scarf, wrapping it in tissue paper and placing it in a gorgeous bag.

"I am. It's been a while since I lived in the Denver area, but I'm glad to be back. And though I don't need a silk scarf, I still want one."

"A girl always needs pretty things." Sierra winked as she told me the total.

I blinked. "I think you have the wrong price. I'm sorry, I thought it was a bit more."

Sierra beamed. "Aren't you an honest one? I truly appreciate that. However, you're getting the welcome home discount. Welcome back to Denver, Brooke."

She handed me the bag after I gave her my credit card, and I tried not to cry. Tears stung my eyes and I swallowed hard. I didn't have any other family. Luke was it for me. No one had said welcome home yet, although Lake and Leif had tried. They had been welcoming, sweet, and yet this just felt different.

"Thank you. Seriously. And I'll be back. I promise."

"That's exactly what I want to hear. Enjoy your day."

I said goodbye to Sierra and made my way down the street, looking at the familiar yet different places that had been here for years, scattered amongst the newer shops and cafés. There was a bookstore that I vaguely remembered had burned down at one point. But they had built it back up, and I figured that I would bring Luke here one day so that he could find a book of his own. Yes, there were probably places closer, but the street called to me.

I looked at a tattoo shop and grinned before nearly tripping over my feet because I knew that name and had to wonder if that was truly connected.

Montgomery Ink?

No, there was no way that this place was connected to all the other Montgomerys. Even though I had a feeling it was. Because Leif told me where his family worked. Spots of conversation and memories hit me again, but I told myself that I was just making things up.

There was no way, in a city as big as Denver, that my life would be this connected to a man I didn't want to think about.

This had to be another tattoo shop that just happened to have his family name on it. I didn't remember the name that he'd used for the shop, just that his last name was Montgomery.

And I was just losing my mind.

Next door was a little café called Taboo. I blinked, wondering if it was a café that was also a burlesque club for some reason, but through the windows I saw baked goods, coffee, and people milling about, enjoying their morning. Since I loved coffee, I figured I would go in and get a cup for myself. I was pretty sure I'd been here before, but then again, I hadn't remembered the name.

I had moved so many times that I seemed to have forgotten some essential things, like the fact that a Montgomery business was right next door.

No, I wasn't going to think about him or his last name.

It was just a coincidence.

A woman with bright red lips and long blond hair stood behind the counter and beamed at me.

"Welcome to Taboo. What can I get you?"

"I would love a vanilla latte. And whatever smells so good," I said with a laugh.

The woman grinned. "That could be a few things, but I did just pull some cinnamon rolls from the oven."

"Did you say cinnamon rolls, Hailey?"

I turned and looked at the open door separating the café from the building next door. A woman with striking dark hair, bright blue eyes, and full sleeves leaned against the doorway.

"I swear, as soon as I allow cinnamon into the air, you just come strolling through, Maya," Hailey said with a laugh.

"It's my curse." The tattooed woman looked at me and grimaced. "I'm sorry for cutting in line. I would say it's my prerogative since we're next door, but that still makes me a jerk. You go ahead. I'll wait in line for my cinnamon rolls."

I laughed, shaking my head. "Well, they do sound amazing, and since they seemed to have drawn you in like a moth to the flame, I'll take one."

"Two cinnamon rolls and two vanilla lattes coming up."

"She knows my drink," Maya said at my questioning look.

"That's sweet," I said, honestly. I liked the fact that this place was so welcoming.

"I'll know your drink soon, too. I always do," Hailey said as she went to work.

I held up my credit card and smiled. "I'll buy hers too. I had a good morning."

"You do *not* have to do that," Maya put in, waving me off.

"Let me. I just moved to the area, and everybody's been so nice to me. I want to be nice back."

The other woman smiled. "Well, thank you. And if

you ever want to tattoo, you should come on over. We would love to have you."

"Aunt Maya, if she wants a tattoo, she's coming to me. Sorry."

I froze, that tingling sensation crawling up my spine. I told myself I would not press my thighs together, swallow hard, or react in any way. I knew that voice, that deep rumble that did things to me that I couldn't think about. Everything twisted in my brain at once as I tried to figure out exactly what happened.

I turned to see Leif standing there, a slight knowing grin on his face. He had pushed his hair back and his beard was a little scruffy. His bright blue eyes were on my face, and I tried not to lick my lips or think about exactly what effect his voice had on me in the past.

I had just had an entire afternoon and dinner with this man, his cousin, and my child. I hadn't reacted in any way then. I wasn't going to do it now. Not in public, and especially not in front of his freaking aunt.

"Oh, it's like that, is it?" Maya asked, laughter in her tone.

"It's not like anything," I blurted, and Leif raised a brow.

"Sure, Brooke. Whatever you say. Though of all the coffee places in the world, you have to walk into mine."

"Oh good, I'm delighted that I get to hear these lines," Maya said with a laugh.

"Your coffee and cinnamon rolls are ready," Hailey said from behind me. I whirled and tried not to trip on my own two feet.

"Oh. Thank you. Seriously. It smells amazing."

"No problem. But you do realize that you will have to tell us how you know our boy here." She winked as she said it, and I swallowed hard.

"Your boy?" I asked, my voice squeaking.

Leif let out a rough chuckle that did bad, bad things to me. "I told you that we Montgomerys take over the world. You just happen to be on our street."

Maya came forward and took her coffee and cinnamon roll as she raised her brow at Leif's words. "Seriously, Brooke, is it? It's nice to meet you. I'm sorry that my nephew here is being a dork and not introducing us properly."

I knew that there were other people in the café, but most weren't paying attention to us. They either had headphones on and were working, or paying attention to what was in front of them rather than the antics of whatever the hell was happening to me.

It was as if they were used to this, and knowing Leif, and how he told tales of the Montgomery family, maybe they were.

"Seriously, is everyone I'm going to bump into

related to you?" I asked, my eyes wide as I looked over at Leif.

"I don't know who you've met yet. And technically, Hailey isn't related to me, but she's an honorary aunt," Leif answered.

"I am an actual aunt," Maya said as she held out her hand. "Maya Montgomery-Gallagher. It's nice to meet you."

I put my hand in hers. "Brooke Adler. It's good to meet you, too. Are you Lake's Mom?" I asked, trying to get the family tree right.

Maya raised a brow. "No, Lake is my cousin's kid. But I think of her as my niece as well. Leif over here is my brother's child. Austin, who owns the shop with me." Maya pointed behind her towards the open door of the tattoo shop. "His mom owns Eden, the boutique across the street."

I looked at the bag with my scarf in it and then up at Leif. "Your mom is that gorgeous woman with auburn hair, isn't she?" I asked, feeling like a poor gazelle surrounded by a pack of Montgomery lions.

Leif grinned. "She is. Dad's not working today because he's off with my siblings at some parent-teacher thing, but Mom is on guard at the shop. I just went to visit her, and she spoke of a lovely woman who was moving back to Denver and had bought a beautiful scarf. She also mentioned that she was pretty, and I should find her and ask her out. Because my mother is constantly trying to get me to settle down," Leif mumbled.

Maya and Hailey both leaned against the counter, staring at us and our byplay.

I let out a slow breath. "I've always loved that shop. You didn't tell me that your mom owned it."

"I want to know what's going on here, but I feel like if I ask anymore, Leif will pull you out of here and I'm never going to know." Maya laughed.

"Brooke and I go way back," Leif explained, and I was glad that was as far as he went. Because nobody else needed to know exactly how far back we went and what happened between us. I still couldn't quite believe it. "She also just moved in next door to Lake."

Maya's eyes widened and she beamed. "Oh, you bought that house, my brothers built it, and my sister did the landscaping."

I shook my head, rubbed my temple, and then took a sip of my latte.

"First, this coffee is amazing. Second, did I just step into a different realm I wasn't aware of? What do you mean your family built it? Or do I want to know?"

Leif laughed. "Some of my family own a construction business, and they just happened to have built part of the neighborhood. Seriously, it's just a coincidence. And you happen to be on the one street in all of Colorado where many of my family members own businesses. I swear you will not run into us in the grocery store or anywhere else around town. You just happened to be where we're mostly congregated."

"You mean on my favorite street in Denver," I mumbled.

"Sweet," Hailey said. She looked over at Maya. "I still have so many questions, but I think that we should leave these two kids alone."

"I guess you're right," Maya said with a sigh. "Thank you for the coffee and cinnamon roll. And I'm serious. If you don't want this big lug over there to do your ink, we would love to have you." She turned to Leif. "Say hello to my boy later, and will we see you this weekend for dinner?"

"You know it. Now I'm going to take Brooke out of here, so she doesn't run away screaming."

"I don't know if that will help," I said with a laugh. I wasn't joking either. I was just trying to keep up with everything.

Then Leif picked up his coffee, that I hadn't even seen him order, and I walked outside next to him, with him holding my bag from Eden and me nibbling on my cinnamon roll as we walked in silence.

"So, your family does own everything here. And all of my favorite spots."

"We own a lot of it. One of my aunts owns that bookshop, and a few of my aunts—that are technically second cousins or something—own places in Boulder, Fort Collins, and Colorado Springs."

I blinked. "How is that even possible?"

Leif shrugged. "I told you that my father had seven siblings, and they all needed jobs. They have lives, and nobody moved away from this area. My uncle Shep moved down to New Orleans at one point, but he moved back up here with his family later on. My cousins have moved around the United States for college and such, but we all end up coming back. This is home." He met my gaze, and I swallowed hard. "You know all about Colorado being home, right?"

"How is this even possible? I met you in Paris, Leif. *Paris*. I know we both said at the time that we were from here, but what are the odds? After all this time. How is this happening?"

I wasn't even going to touch on the fact that I was still bitter. Still angry. It had nothing to do with what happened in the past five years. Nothing to do with Luke's father, my new job, or the reason for moving.

No, it had all to do with what happened after Paris. Or rather, what hadn't happened.

"I don't know, Brooke. This is just my home. I don't know what else to think." He was standing in front of me, and I hadn't even realized his fingers were touching my skin, trailing along my jaw.

"Leave." It was the only thing I could say.

"Brooke."

"I don't know what to do."

He hadn't shown at the time, hadn't met me as we had promised.

I should be angry, push away, and forget everything that happened. But I wasn't that little girl anymore. I wasn't a teenager who thought she was an adult. I *was* an adult, a single mom, and I wanted to know him.

That was the problem with Leif Montgomery. I had always wanted to know him.

So when he lowered his head to mine and pressed a soft kiss against my lips, it was as if everything came back in a heartbeat. Memories of who we were and what we thought we wanted out of life assailed me.

"Just like I remember," he whispered.

I swallowed hard, licked my lips, and stepped back. "I'm not that person anymore, Leif. A lot of things have changed."

He studied my face and I wondered what I meant by that. What did I want? I wanted a new life, a change. That was why I moved here.

Leif might be part of my past, but he wasn't part of the past I was leaving.

I just didn't know what that meant, and since everything was so confusing, I needed to breathe first. To take things slow. To make a list, go through all of my options and then decide. That was the only way I could function.

"Welcome home, Brooke."

"To the same home you've always been," I whispered.

"I'm not going anywhere, Brooke. I never did."

"Are you sure about that?" I asked.

But he didn't answer, and I wasn't sure that he could. So we stood there on a busy street, one filled with so many memories, and yet, somehow, they were all tangled with Leif. I just hadn't known it. Once again, I stood on a precipice, waiting to fall.

Knowing the landing could only ever end in heartbreak.

Chapter 5

Brooke

I INHALED THE SCENT OF BOOKS, THAT FAMILIAR essence that settled me, and held back a smile. In another life, I would have been a librarian. Being surrounded by books soothed me, whether they were fiction, nonfiction, reference, or something unique.

I wasn't a librarian, though. No, as of today, I was a physics professor at Denver State University, DSU. Nuclear physics was my expertise, something I had gravitated towards in undergrad at this very university. I graduated here with my bachelor's in physics. I then had ended up at MIT for my doctorate before heading to the California Institute of Technology, also known as Caltech, for my postdoc and eventual job.

I had been a Pasadena girl for the past couple of years and enjoyed my job as a professor, researcher, and nuclear physicist, but it was nice to come home.

I had walked these hallowed halls as an undergrad, a teenager, and a young twentysomething, trying to figure out my place in the world.

And now here I was again, thirty years old, a single mom, and feeling slightly more lost than I had been when I first took the job in this tenure-track position.

"We're so happy that you're here," Patrice said as she smiled at me.

The older woman with dark hair, a kind smile, yet shrewd eyes nodded at me. "Not only is it nice to have another woman in the physics department, but your breadth of research is also quite illuminating."

I looked over at Dr. Patrice Robbins and smiled softly. "I'm glad that there is another woman in the department, as well. Whenever I work with the chemistry department, I usually get to work alongside more women, and with each passing year, there are more and more women in science, but you're right, there is a lack in most physics circles."

"Well, you're not alone here. And now it is not just me at this level, though there are many women in the associate track, postdocs, and students. We're all happy to have you." Her eye twitched for a second, and I wondered if she truly meant *everyone* was happy to have me.

Because it was my experience that not everybody liked when a younger woman stepped into such a high-powered job in academia. I was younger than most of my counterparts and had finished my degrees in fewer years than some. I was good at what I did, and I was smart. I was also very blessed with my childcare opportunities. When I lost Luke's father before Luke was even born, I hadn't been forced to put my dreams aside while caring for my infant son.

I had still somehow been able to do it all, although I don't remember sleeping those first two years.

"I'm excited to get started. I know I'm the newbie, so any help and advice you have, I'm here for it."

"I know we've been talking about lesson plans, and physics 102 you will be teaching this semester starting next week, so you're already ahead of the game on that. And the head of the department is excited to hear about it, too."

"I had a meeting with him just before this. I know he's off to speak with the President of the University for one of their board meetings, so he's a very busy man."

"He does the work of two people, but I so appreciate him. He listens to what his professors need, and more importantly, he listens to the students."

I smiled at that. "That sounds like a great place to

start."

"Glad to hear it. Now, you can set up your office however you want. You know how to do office hours and what classes you will be teaching this semester. We can discuss next year's classes soon, as well. I know you are going to want to get started on your research team, any grad classes that you're working on next semester, and postdocs and graduate students you plan to take on."

I nodded, knowing the drill. I had done similar work at Caltech, though now I was in a more prominent position.

"I've been working on those plans and speaking with everyone through email and phone calls for the past three months, so I'm ready to go."

"Good, and of course, there's the social aspect of our job." She rolled her eyes and I held back a laugh, even as tension slid into me.

"Social aspect?" I asked, suddenly afraid that because we were the women in this position, we would be in charge of setting up parties and dinners for faculty.

She held up her hand. "No, not that."

"Was it all over my face?" I asked, laughing now.

"A little bit. I thought the same thing when I started here a few years ago. But you were here as an undergrad, though I was in the chemistry department then, so I don't remember teaching you. I'm sorry."

I shook my head. "I don't think we crossed paths. So, what do you mean by social?" I asked, knowing that I had a few things to do, and I wanted to get home to see Luke soon. Not to mention I was going to do my best not to think about Leif Montgomery and that kiss.

No matter what happened, I could not think about that kiss.

Even if I could still taste him on my lips, feel the tingling sensation that wouldn't go away.

No, I would not think about him.

"Our department chair wants us to be more of a 'family' than a workplace." I wasn't sure if Patrice agreed with what she said, but she wasn't rolling her eyes as she said it, so I figured it might be a good thing.

"Okay? What does that entail?"

"That means if you have a problem or need to talk to someone about anything, work, students, paperwork, anything related to that, you go to your department chair or anyone you feel comfortable with within the department. We don't want you to feel like you're all alone and new at this. We've all had a few more years of experience than you, but that doesn't mean what you bring isn't beneficial." She let out a breath. "I'm saying this all wrong because there's the party line of wanting you to feel comfortable, and me as a person telling you that I'm excited that you're here. And that if you have a problem with anyone in the department, come to me, and I'll help."

I froze, a little worried about what she was saying.

"Am I going to have a problem with someone in the department?" I asked, my voice low.

We were in my office now, a smallish rectangle of a room with bookshelves, a desk, and a couple of chairs. I would spruce it up and make it my own soon, someplace I could work, study, and bring students in, but right now it just felt like an empty box.

Patrice closed the door behind her, and trepidation filled me.

"You were the best candidate for the job, and every single one of us, bar one, is excited that you're here. You are in a tenure-track position, and this university will do great with you."

"But?" I asked, my voice a little sharper than intended.

"There is another associate professor named Landon Cunning who might make trouble."

I froze; that name sounded far too familiar for my own liking. "As in President Cunning? The former president of the university when I was a student?" I asked, pieces clicking into place.

Patrice cringed. "Yes. His son's an associate professor now and wanted your job."

I rubbed my temples. "Great. Let me guess, Landon has made it known that he wanted this job and isn't happy that I'm here?"

"Pretty much. He's very smooth about his desire for it as well. He's not going to do anything to damage your reputation or the reputation of this school. But he is going to be an asshole. Sorry for my language."

"Don't be sorry about your language. I curse more than that."

Patrice's eyes filled with laughter. "I have a feeling we could be good friends, Brooke."

"It sounds like I could use one. I have to ask though, if you don't think he will hurt my reputation or this school, why are you warning me?"

"Because he can be intimidating and a jerk. And I don't want you to be blindsided because he wanted your job and didn't get it. You were the one who was more qualified. You have the better research grants and the broader ideas for the university. You know just as well as I do that Harvard and MIT are ranked number one and two in physics in the United States. You left Caltech, which was ranked third. You could have done extraordinary things there. I know you could have. But you came here, and we are tied with Stanford at fourth in physics." Patrice gave me a grin. "It is my goal to beat Stanford, so we will no longer be tied, and maybe one day hit third while we're at it."

"That would be nice." I let out a breath. "I didn't leave Caltech because I didn't think they were as good as here or wanted greener pastures. I came here because the department gave me what I needed and will need, and this is where I grew up. I wanted to come home. Meaning I want this university to thrive

with me here. And I want to thrive as well. It's good to
know that I will have some bumpy roads ahead, but at
least I know where they're coming from."

I didn't think it would come from the woman in
front of me. She had warned me right off the bat that
somebody had wanted my job, especially because this
Landon was the son of the former president of the
university. The president had retired because he had
felt like it, rather than being pushed out for some
scandal or something. So at least I counted that better
than an issue that could have arisen. However, I was
still worried. I had enough on my plate rather than
worrying about some guy who didn't like that I got the
job he wanted.

Worst case, he thought I got it just because I was a
woman and I was needed to reach their "quota." Best
case, he would get over it once he realized that I was a
hard worker, good at what I did, and was going to
bring good things to this university.

I just hoped I was given a chance.

I didn't like feeling as if I might not fit in already,
and I hadn't even met the other professors, other than
during my interviews and through online meetings.

Patrice left me after walking me to my lab, a place
filled with a few items from the previous professor, but
now I would make my own.

I rolled my shoulders back and turned as the door
opened and my team walked in.

I had chosen my team without ever having met them in person. Coming in as a professor trying to build a team for papers and books and research that would help the world of nuclear physics wasn't easy. I wasn't bringing anyone with me, as some people did. My former professor had actually brought the postdoc with them as a former grad student, and at least they'd had a ready-made team with the two of them.

I was starting nearly from scratch.

"Hi there, Dr. Adler," Randall said as he set down his messenger bag. Randall was my postdoc, who had a year left under his contract before he would start looking for jobs, in the private sector, industry, or as an associate professor at some other university. He could do many things once he left this university and his place with me, but for the next year, he was my partner.

"You can call me Brooke while it's the group of us," I said as I smiled at the rest of my team.

Jennifer was a fourth-year grad student who had worked under the previous professor, and instead of moving to a group that could have accommodated her so she could finish her previous research, she decided to work with me. My research didn't follow the same path that hers had, but I was going to tailor-fit what she had been working on with what I had so that she could develop a doctoral thesis and presentation within the next two years. If she had been a fifth-year grad, I would have hoped her professor would have at least waited for her to graduate, but thankfully we didn't have to deal with that.

She and Randall would be the leaders for my team.

Randall would also be working with me for my class since it was a team effort to make sure that a GEN Ed class of introductory physics, which had over three hundred students per class, actually knew what they were doing.

The last remaining member of my team was Hannah, a second-year grad who had changed focus after the previous year.

"Hello, Jennifer and Hannah," I said, going to my laboratory desk. "I know we haven't been here that long, but I am excited that we will be working together."

"It's good to see you in person," Jennifer said as she sat down at her desk.

"I totally agree," Hannah added.

"I know I missed the introductions to the next wave of grad students that are going to be coming here in the next week, but soon they're going to be doing the rounds where we will get to put on our best faces and hope that they want to work with us in the lab."

"Of course they are going to want to work with us. We're going to kick ass," Jennifer said with a grin.

"That's what I want to hear. I know we already went over a few things that we're going to start next week, and I have about forty-five minutes before I need to head home. So, do you guys have any questions?"

"So, you don't expect us to stay too late every evening?" Hannah asked.

I shook my head. "As long as the work gets done and we are there for each other when we need to be, I don't expect you to work until one in the morning. And I'm going to be honest, all three of you know that I'm a single mom. I may have help, but I can't expect her to stay overnight so that I can get some research done that would be better served after a few hours of sleep and lots of coffee."

All three of them nodded as we went over the next steps of what we needed to do in the next couple of weeks. I was going to ensure that everybody that worked for me understood that being able to sleep during grad school led to better decisions. I didn't want my students in undergrad or grad school to be strung out, unhealthy, exhausted, and a mess to be around.

Luke was also my first priority, beyond my career or anything I was doing in the physics world. He knew that, and my team would soon know that if they hadn't already figured it out. If anybody had a problem that I was a single mom, they were going to have to deal with it.

But, so far, things were working out. We went over a checklist, and I knew I would be emailing them soon, but for now I wanted to get home and see my kiddo.

Once we were done in the lab, I followed them out to my office to gather my things. I'd spent the morning downtown, reliving my youth and memories that continued to assail me, the afternoon getting Luke from kindergarten, set up with his nanny, and getting settled at DSU. This evening I would spend time with my favorite person in the world. And not think about Leif. Apparently, I wasn't doing a very good job about that because it was all I was thinking about. Over and over and over again.

I slid my belongings into my leather bag, grabbed my purse, and headed toward my door.

A man in trim slacks, a dark Henley, and a wicked grin leaned against my doorway. His chestnut hair was longish, a lock of it trailing over his forehead. He had deep-green eyes and slight stubble over his chin.

He also did nothing for me, unlike Leif.

Well, crap.

"Brooke, correct?" the man in front of me asked, and I did my best not to stiffen. Because now I knew exactly who this was.

"Dr. Adler, yes. You must be Dr. Cunning." I held up my hand, and he looked down at it for a minute before giving me a tight and formal handshake.

"You can call me Landon if you'd like. I can call you Dr. Adler if that is what you prefer."

I grinned at him and tried not to feel weird. To be honest, he would've creeped me out just with the way he was looking at me, even without Patrice's warning. But because I had been forewarned, I wasn't going to let him get away with trying to put me off my stride.

"You know us, doctors, we spent so much time trying to get those letters, we tend to like them. But I can call you whatever you'd like. Landon or Dr. Cunning."

"I guess going by doctors works. Although if anyone asks us if we know a doctor while we're sitting in a restaurant and somebody's choking, they better not look to us, right?"

"Hazards of the job, I guess. Anyway, I'm headed out. It is so nice to meet you. I'm sure I'll see you around the halls."

He looked at my office with a proprietary gaze, and I wanted to kick him out, but I had to be better than him. I needed to show him that I was the person for this job and that he didn't have to act like a peacock strutting down the hallway. It was the only way to get things done. It was what I had learned in every situation I had ever been in when someone didn't feel like I was qualified for the place I was in.

He would learn that I was far smarter than he thought I was. And that I wasn't the bitch he wanted me to be.

"Let me take you out for a drink." He grinned, acting so smooth, as if I hadn't seen that anger in his gaze for an instant. "To welcome you to the university."

"I need to head home, but thank you. Maybe a group of us can go out for drinks soon."

There was no way I would be going out for a drink alone with this man. Ever.

"Sounds like a plan. I'll see you around, Brooke, I mean, Dr. Adler." He winked before he strolled away, going to talk with an older professor with salt-and-pepper hair that I recognized from the chemistry department from when I was a student.

I shook my head and told myself I just imagined the hostility even though I knew I hadn't, even a little bit.

Not the perfect way to start my first day, but considering it wasn't my first full day at the university, I wasn't going to count this.

I made my way to my car and headed home, knowing that May and Luke would be waiting for me. I pulled past May's car into my garage, and practically threw myself out of my SUV, wanting to see Luke. Though I had worked long hours before, and it wasn't as if this was the first time he had ever been with a caretaker other than me, we had been spending so much time together lately. I just wanted to see my little boy. Yes, I had seen him after his half-day of school so I could hug him right as soon as he got out, but it was only for a few moments before I had had to go to work and leave him alone without me.

I missed my little boy, and I hated not being able to be with him every single moment of every single day.

But hopefully, I would get better at this.

Or at least get back into the hang of it.

"Mommy!" Luke called as he ran to me. I went down to my knees, tossed my things on the floor, and hugged him close, inhaling that little boy scent that was all my son.

He started talking a mile a minute about his afternoon with May as if I hadn't seen him a couple of hours ago. For some reason, my eyes stung, and I swallowed hard before I looked up at the woman with straight black hair, green eyes, and a sweet smile.

May waved. "Today has gone amazing. I'm so happy that we're having as much fun as we are. I can go over exactly what happened today, or maybe we can do that tomorrow? That way you can have the rest of the evening with the kiddo?"

It was as if she read my mind. Yes, I wanted to go through everything in detail because I was that anal-retentive, and I knew it would be helpful for our relationship, so we were always on the same page. But I also wanted time with my son.

So I nodded, said my goodbyes as May hugged Luke tight, and then I sat down on the floor right next to my son and heard about his day in detail once again, and knew that even though this had been a hard decision, it had been the best one.

Even though I had no family here, no connections, it was better for us to move back to Colorado.

Luke was my family, my connection.

When we heated up dinner—casserole thanks to Lake—I couldn't help but think of Leif, and the fact that Montgomerys seemed to be closing ranks around me, even though they hadn't meant to, and I hadn't even realized it was happening. Everywhere I went, I seemed to bump into a Montgomery. There were probably a couple at the university for all I knew. Either as students or professors. I would have to check into that.

Or I could just ignore it because it didn't matter.

Of course, my phone lit up at that moment, an unfamiliar number gracing the screen.

Unknown number: *This is Leif. You gave me your number all those years ago, and I kept it. I hope this is still you.*

I swallowed hard. I had ignored the texts between us all those years ago because I'd been so angry. And deleted his contact information.

I never blocked him.

Luke was coloring in his favorite superhero coloring book, and I knew that I only had a few minutes before I had to get him ready for bed, but I swallowed hard and picked up my phone.

Me: *It's still me.*

Leif: *You have no idea how happy I am to hear that. I was really worried I was texting a random stranger.*

Me: *I don't know. It's been a few years. I feel like a stranger.*

I hadn't even meant to type that, but there was no going back now. Leif Montgomery just did that to me.

Leif: *I would like to get to know you. I know that's a line, and I could probably come up with something better, to flirt better, but I don't know. I felt the connection today. And we keep bumping into each other. That has to mean something. That's not a line. Can I take you out? I know you're busy with your new life, with Luke, but let me take you out.*

I should say no. I should walk away and forget him. Just like I had been trying to forget him for ten years.

I had been doing a pretty damn good job of it too, until I moved back and met up with him again.

Not once, but twice.

There was no escaping Leif Montgomery, especially not when his cousin lived next door.

If I said no now, what would happen? Would I stop thinking about him? No, I didn't think that was possible.

So I did the only thing that made sense to me.

I let out a breath and answered.

Me: *Okay.*

I hoped this time I wouldn't break when it all crashed down around me.

Chapter 6

Leif

MONTGOMERY INK LEGACY'S ONE-YEAR ANNIVERSARY was coming up, yet it still felt like opening day had been just yesterday.

Our shop wasn't downtown, surrounded by extraordinary architecture and busy necessities. But we did have the mountains as our backdrop and trees surrounding us, though we were technically in a strip mall.

My aunt and uncle's place down in Colorado Springs was also in a strip mall right off the highway. Our legacy establishment at least had trees surrounding us. It didn't make it any easier for us to not compare ourselves to the original shop in down-town Denver, but that was something I did every day anyway, even if my family didn't.

The original Montgomery Ink had a few cosmetic changes over time. It had once been bright hot pink and black with chrome, then had gone a little more subtle, and then went back to nearly princess goth, according to my cousin.

Now it looked like a professional art-house with a similar feel to my place. Not because I wanted to emulate my parents, but because we had similar taste.

When I was younger, I tried to figure out what I wanted to be. Who I want to be. I had tried to figure out exactly *where* I wanted to find myself. I thought I'd be an artist of some sort because that's what I loved. At one point, I thought I would go to culinary school, but no, art in some fashion had been for me.

When I was trying to figure out what I wanted to do, Lake had come to me with an idea. She was an investor, a brilliant woman who had her own tech company and made a shit ton of money. She constantly put that back into other women-owned busi-nesses but wanted something of her own that was family-driven.

So she and I decided to do something with it. I had saved and scrimped for the past ten years or so, working at my dad's shop, then down in New Orleans at my uncle's old place, and countless other sites learning art and getting experience. That's why I had gone to Paris all those years ago.

When the time came for a new branch of Montgomery Ink to open, Lake and I had come up with a plan. And then my best friend Nick had wanted in, had saved up as well, and had wanted to be a full partner.

He might not be a Montgomery, but in my heart, he was. And frankly, with how much time he spent with my family and how he'd practically lived with us when we were kids, he was a Montgomery.

Sebastian was our fourth partner, or at least he *would* be. He still needed to finish college, something he wanted to do, not just for his parents, and had a few more years of apprenticeship ahead of him, but when the time came, he was going to buy into our branch as well.

As we had come up with this plan as a group of four, we had gone to my father and aunt to discuss how we could make this happen.

That was two years ago, and now here I was today, sitting in my booth, going over sketches for my next client. All while trying not to feel like I was failing because I wasn't living up to anyone's expectations.

Not that those expectations were put on me by anyone but myself. It was complicated, and I hated that my mind kept doing this. I'd lived ten years of twisted shit in my brain before becoming a Montgomery.

Those years didn't just fade away, despite trying to bury them for as long as I had.

"Okay, get it out," my best friend said from the booth beside me, and I narrowed my gaze at him.

"What?" I asked, though I knew that Nick could read my mind like no other. It should probably bother me that Nick knew me better than my siblings did, but my siblings were a lot younger than me. I loved my brothers and sister. They were everything to me. But Nick and I bonded from the moment we first met. There was no changing that bond.

The only other person I was as close to was Lake, and she hadn't come into my life until years later. My cousin and I had just clicked, and we hadn't been apart since.

"I think Nick is wondering why you are growling to yourself as you draw," Tristan clarified as he worked on a floral piece on his client's ribs.

"Maybe he's thinking about his date tonight," Taryn added, her lips twitching into a smile.

"Oh, so he finally asked her out? I missed that part." Leo ran his hands through his hair and grinned up at me. "Congrats, man."

I glared at my friends and coworkers and shook my head. "You guys know far too much about me. I don't like it."

"They just like you," Tristan's client said from

where she lay face-down on the bench, her eyes closed in peace as if she wasn't getting a tattoo.

I loved that nearly every woman who came in for a tattoo either smiled, held an entire conversation, or fell asleep. It was often the big beefy guys who were assholes to us, talking about the little women who couldn't handle pain, who were usually the ones that screamed the loudest.

That always made me smile.

"What did I miss?" Sebastian asked as he walked through the door, Lake right behind him.

I shook my head, laughing now. "We're a full house here, and everybody's up in my business."

"Oh, about your date with Brooke?" Lake asked as she walked toward the back office, her high heels echoing off the walls.

We had painted the place soft cream with white trim. That way, we could add artwork and other pieces to personalize each individual station. Lake had wanted to go gold with the fixtures, with funky lighting and chandeliers to make it look elegant and yet artsy at the same time. I had gone along with it since she knew better than I did, and the guys had agreed.

We had a set of offices in the back where we did a lot of the paperwork, and Lake was there more often than I was. I had a business degree and had gotten it so I could do exactly this, but Lake enjoyed that part.

Since she was the one that was a master with money and tech, I let her do it.

She leaned against the wall, slid off her high heels, let out a groan, and then slid on a pair of flats that she kept here.

"I don't understand why you wear those high heels if you just come here and take them off. Why didn't you take them off in the car? Why wear them at all?" Nick asked, grumbling.

The two were friends, business partners, and adversaries. They always rubbed each other the wrong way, and yet I knew they would do anything for each other. Just like I would for either of them.

Lake gave him her prim and proper gaze, and I held back a laugh. Nick hated when she did that. It just made me smile.

"I've been wearing heels all day, and I *can* constantly wear them, but I wasn't in the mood. I like how my legs look in them, so get over yourself, Nick."

"Ooh," Tristan, Taryn, and Leo cheered simultaneously.

I looked at Sebastian and we shook our heads before he came to sit next to me and look over what I was doing. Sebastian and I knew better than to egg the two of them on in their bickering. It wasn't like they were truly fighting. They just enjoyed the push.

Nick growled. "I was just wondering why you were

hurting yourself. Far be it for me to talk about women's fashion."

"You really shouldn't be talking about women's fashion," Taryn said with a laugh.

"Fine." Nick rolled his eyes. I looked over at Sebastian.

"How was class today?" I asked, and Sebastian rubbed the back of his neck.

"Fine. I know I need a degree because I want to learn how to help take care of the business, but it's a little weird already knowing what I'm going to do for the rest of my life while a lot of my friends in college are trying to figure out where is the best place to party."

My cousin sometimes seemed older than his years, but it also made me sad because he should be able to go out to party to have fun.

"Are you going out with your girlfriend at all? Beyond your old people dates?"

"Old people dates?" Lake asked as she walked forward, looking over a stack of papers.

"He's just being a jerk. I do not go on old people dates."

"You guys went to a stamp collection *event* last week," I said dryly.

"That's a thing?" Nick asked.

Sebastian held out his hands. "I'm eighteen. I can't drink. Not that I'm sure I even want to. And Marley wanted to see if it was fun." He gave me a dry look. "It was not fun."

I laughed, shaking my head. "You love that girl something fierce."

Sebastian grinned. "I do. And one day, she's going to be my wife."

Leo coughed into his fist. "You're eighteen, man. I understand young love and all that, but have you dated anyone other than her?"

Sebastian shook his head. "No, but why should I have to date other people to know that Marley is it for me?"

"Childhood loves can be the sweetest thing," Lake put in.

"Really? How's that guy Deke that you dated in high school?" Nick asked.

In answer, Lake flipped him off. "Go to hell."

"Already there, babe."

The two went at it again. I sighed.

"They should just make out already," Sebastian grumbled, and I held back a laugh.

"I think they would kill each other if they ever dated. Plus, Lake is dating that guy. Zach."

Sebastian shook his head. "The guy from that double date?"

"Same guy. He seems good for her. Or at least she's happy. And Nick and Lake just like butting heads. Not every frenemy you have turns into something more."

"Well, if that isn't an ominous saying, I don't know what is." Sebastian grinned, then looked over my work. "You have an appointment later today?"

"Tomorrow. I'm just getting everything prepped because I'm going out with Brooke tonight."

"So, tell us about this Brooke. I hear she's the one that you dated in Paris."

I scowled over at Lake. "Did you tell everybody?"

"Maybe." My cousin raised her chin. "Or maybe I just told the crew here when you weren't looking."

"Don't you dare tell my parents," I growled.

"Oh, they already know." Sebastian beamed.

I scowled over at my cousin. "What?"

"You practically claimed her in front of Aunt Maya and Hailey. Of course, the family knows. Now we're all invested in this relationship with Brooke. I'm surprised it took you this long to ask her out."

"Dear God," I grumbled.

"It's your fault for laying claim to her inside the family café," Lake warned.

"With that logic, there's no place safe in the state of Colorado when it comes to you Montgomerys," Nick complained.

"That is true. It's why I'll never date a Montgomery, and I always ask for someone's birth records before I go out with them." Leo laughed, his eyes twinkling.

I rolled my eyes. "You guys are hilarious. I'm so

happy that we're sitting here discussing dating my family, not working."

"You're just salty because we're all interested in your relationship," Lake teased. "Seriously though, make this work because I want to go on a double date."

"We all know how well the double date with you worked out last time." I crossed my eyes.

"It's not my fault it didn't work. That just means you were waiting for Brooke." She rolled her eyes and went back to the office to work. I scowled at my family and friends and did the same, knowing that I needed to head home and get ready soon.

I had a date with Brooke tonight, and I knew this was my last chance.

At what?

I didn't know.

But some part of me wanted to find out.

Chapter 7

Leif

BROOKE WANTED TO MEET ME AT THE RESTAURANT, rather than having me pick her up. Honestly, I was shocked she had even agreed to the date in the first place, so I wasn't going to be picky about it. She had a kid to worry about, and though I had been in her house, and knew where she lived, there were boundaries. And I understood them.

But I still wanted to know why.

Why she'd given up on us before we had even had a chance all those years ago.

Had she found someone else? Well, clearly, she had because she was a mom, after all. But had she found someone else right after Paris? While we were still in Paris?

Had she realized that she wanted someone different and I wasn't it?

Our time in Paris had meant something to me.

Clearly, it had meant something different to her, and maybe tonight we would actually figure out what that was.

Or we could move on from who we had been, something I was trying to do now that I wasn't a teenager or twentysomething anymore. Maybe ignoring our pasts and moving on was the best bet. She had said yes to this date, after all—that counted for something.

And I was going to make sure it did because I needed it to.

I wanted her, and I wanted to see what could happen if we finally did take that chance.

I pulled into the casual American cuisine restaurant and got out of the car, not at all surprised to see that Brooke was already there. She stood by the entrance in a pretty dress, high heels, and frowned down at her phone. That little V between her brows deepened and I wondered if she was worried about something, or if she was already regretting this.

I cleared my throat. "I should have remembered that you like to be earlier than anybody else. I'm sorry I'm late."

Brooke looked up, her eyes wide, and she slid her phone into her purse and smiled at me.

My heart sped up with that smile. I got lost in those eyes, and it was hard for me to even think.

She had always done that to me, and here she was, doing it again.

"I'm just perpetually early. My sitter and Luke were having such a grand old time, that they didn't need me to stay and interrupt their evening any longer than I was." She rolled her eyes, grinning. She wasn't worried about the sitter spending so much time with her kid that it changed her dynamic. She was self-assured when she came to being a mother; I liked that about her.

"Luke's a great kid, I could see why he gets along with everybody that he meets."

Brooke beamed as if I had told her that she just won a million dollars. "He really is the best. And he loves his nanny already. I was a little worried about starting off a whole new relationship when we moved out here, but they clicked right away, and I'm forever grateful for her."

"I'm glad that you're able to get childcare worked out."

I gestured towards the restaurant, placed my hand at the small of her back, and tried to ignore the warmth emanating off of her as she stiffened ever so slightly, before relaxing into my touch.

I counted that as a win because she hadn't pulled away. I might've surprised her, but she wasn't pulling away.

"I'm glad that I was able to work everything out as well. The school has some childcare, but not exactly what I wanted. I never want Luke to feel like a burden."

I nodded and gave my name to the hostess as she looked for our reservation. We followed the woman quickly to the table. I sat across from Brooke, trying not to get lost in her eyes, and to remember what we were talking about.

"My family decided around the time that they were all having kids to create a childcare facility for all the Montgomerys. It started off as a room in the back of the tattoo shop and turned into something a bit bigger. With so many cousins, it made sense. Now there are Montgomery family childcare services in four cities."

Brooke leaned forward, grinning. "Is it just for Montgomerys? Or do you guys have an actual business for people with Montgomery connections?"

"We're a business, in that we have all the paperwork and it is legal, but really only family and friends of the Montgomerys, and those who work for Montgomery-owned businesses can keep their kids there. We're talking about more than a dozen or so kids at a time, especially back when all my siblings were younger. I don't think they could handle much more."

Brooke's eyes widened and she shook her head. "All I have is Luke, so it's kind of unimaginable that you have so many family members. Though I felt that way when we first met. You had this huge family, and I had only had my parents."

Something crossed her features, and I wasn't sure I was ready to dive too deep into all that pain and loss. And from the way that she closed up, neither was she. I had to keep this casual at first, go slow.

As in, don't scare her with promises of forever because I wasn't sure that's what I had to offer. I had to make sure that's what either of us would want in the first place.

"I still can't believe I said yes," Brooke blurted, and I threw my head back and laughed.

I noticed a few stares our way, but I shrugged them off. I was used to people staring. I was a big guy, had tattoos and piercings, and grew up with people who had even more than I did.

Staring was the usual.

"Honestly, I'm surprised you said yes." I grinned as I said it, and she smiled right back before looking contemplative.

"What are we doing?" she asked.

I didn't have a chance to answer because our waiter was there, taking our order. By the time they were gone, Brooke was staring at me, her gaze nervous.

"I wanted to take you out to dinner, Brooke. There's something here. You can feel it, can't you?"

I wasn't good about being open like this, honest. But it felt like I had known Brooke forever, not just I had known her forever ago.

"I don't know, Leif. I'm just trying to get my life in order. Start a new career, be a good mom. I don't know if I have time for dating."

I looked around. "We have time right now. Have a delicious dinner. You tell me about your work, I'll tell you about mine. If we start talking about my family, that will take hours, and there you go, a whole date."

Brooke's brows rose. "You think a date is going to take hours?"

I smiled; I couldn't help it. "If you do it right."

"You're ridiculous, Montgomery."

"I try. No seriously, tell me about work. Luke. Anything." I paused. "Wait. What if you don't want to talk about Luke? Is he off-limits? I understand if he is. I've never actually dated a single mom before."

She gave me a small smile, playing with the edge of her water glass. "I haven't dated much as a single mom."

"Can you talk about his father?" I hadn't meant to ask that because I figured it was a touchy subject. I had just said we could talk about anything else and to keep things from getting complicated. Yet here I was, making things complicated.

"Luke's father passed away." She let out a breath as I reached forward and gripped her hand.

"I'm sorry. Let's talk about anything else. Let's talk about cheese." I blurted out the first thing that came to mind, and since I was Montgomery, of course it was cheese.

Brooke's eyes widened before she burst out laughing. "I had forgotten your love of cheese. Okay, we're not surrounded by French cheeses, so I know you must be sad, but let's talk about cheese."

I shook my head. "If that's what you want." My lips twitched, as did hers.

She met my gaze, then shrugged. "I never married Henry, Luke's father. He was an English professor, and quite a bit older than me. We had a glorious affair, that was never meant to last, and then I got pregnant." She shrugged, but I knew there's a lot more to that. "I was in my twenties, he was nearly forty."

My brows rose. "Are you serious?"

She gave me a defiant look, even though I saw the hurt in them. "I was an adult, making my own choices, but he was having a midlife crisis, and I was letting myself have fun for the first time in a long while. Either way, I got Luke out of the deal. When I was heading into my third trimester, Henry was killed in a botched robbery attempt. They found the guy. He's in jail now and will be for a long, long time. But Henry never got to meet his son, and Luke never got to meet his father."

She let out a slow breath. "I was never going to marry Henry. But we would've been good friends raising him. And that is my tragic story. I'm a single mom with no parents, with no one. But I moved back to Colorado because I wanted a new chance to live life to its fullest, in a place that I used to love. In a place that I want my son to love. California worked for us before, but the job that I have now at the university is going to bring more opportunities for me and my son. And that's all that matters."

I reached out once more, gripped her hand, and squeezed. "I'm sorry. That you went through all of that, and that you have to explain all of that to random dudes you go on dates with. I'm sorry that Luke lost him. I'm sorry that you did, too."

She met my gaze again, smiling softly. "I know you lost your mom at a young age and didn't find your father until you were older, so I know you sort of have an idea what Luke is dealing with. But he is strong, and I remind him of his father as much as I can, even though they never met. I'm trying to give him everything that I possibly can. That way he never feels like he's lacking anything."

"I know you, Brooke. Or, at least, I knew you before. I'm starting to know the woman in front of me. You would never make him feel like he's missing out on anything. You're doing everything you can for him."

"You can tell that from just looking at me?" she asked, studying my face.

"Maybe. Or maybe I can just tell. Who knows." I let out a breath. "My mom was an okay mom. I know it's probably not the greatest thing to say about someone who's no longer here. But as I remember the years that I had with her, I know that she wasn't the best mom."

Perhaps this wasn't the best conversation for a first date, but Brooke knew some of it, and we had a past. A history. We weren't starting at square one here.

"Mom drank a lot, did some pot, did a few things that weren't pot. She liked what she liked, and liked who she liked, and sometimes that wasn't me."

"Leif."

I shook my head. "No, I don't mind talking about it. I spoke about it with my family and with therapists numerous times." I let out a breath, even as I gave her a self-deprecating smile.

"My mom hid my existence from my dad because she felt like it. Because she wanted the power, and she didn't want to share me. She might have made up reasons later for him, but they were lies. It didn't matter that she had been dating my dad, and even though my dad had always said that they were casual, he never would've just left me alone with her. As soon as he realized I existed, he dropped everything for me."

Brooke pressed her lips together, as if she wanted to say something, but held back.

"He went through all the legal hassles and paperwork in order to keep me, even though I had run away from CPS that day, hitching rides in order to get downtown to see him. It made no sense, and I was an idiot ten-year-old, but he took me in." I smiled at her. "So did my mom, Sierra."

"Your dad's wife?"

I shook my head. "Not at the time. They were only dating. Or, I don't even know if they were really dating then. Maybe just like one date or something. But she was there when I showed up, and she hasn't gone away since." I cringed. "I call her Mom, and most of the time I think she's a better mom to me than my mom had ever been. I know for damn sure she's a good mom to my three siblings. And I feel bad about saying that because my birth mom is gone."

My birth mom had done things that even my dad didn't know, he never needed to know. My dad had enough guilt about all that time he lost as it was. He didn't need anything else on his massive shoulders.

Brooke was quiet for a moment, as if she were trying to formulate a response. "You do have an abundance of family; I'm glad that you have them."

"I am, too. And Luke will always be happy he has you." I smiled then, thinking of my family and all they did for me. I tried to be the best son for them, to give back. I wasn't always, but I figured my track record was better than it could have been.

"You never going to answer what we're doing, are you?" she asked, after the waiter set down our food.

I looked at my plate, and then up at her, meeting her gaze. "I don't know what I'm doing. I know that you need to find your roots, to be a good mom, but you can do that while having dinner with me, Brooke. Because I want to kiss you again. I want to see you again. But if I'm going to scare you by saying things like that, you have to let me know now."

I wasn't sure why I was saying any of this. Not when I had shit to do that could crumble everything, but I had told myself I was going to try. Try to go out and have a future that wasn't just me working for hours upon hours. I tried that with my blind date, and yet here was Brooke, my past coming back with a vengeance. I didn't ask her about why she hadn't come before, after Paris. Why she was here now.

This wasn't the time for that.

It would be, soon.

"You confound me, Leif Montgomery. You make me want to say things and do things that I know I do not have time for."

I smirked. "It's what I'm best at, babe."

"Don't call me babe." Her eyes filled with laughter as she said it, though, so I grinned.

"Whatever you say, babe."

FOR THE REST OF OUR DINNER, WE STAYED ON SAFE topics: work, friends, and Lake.

When I walked her to her car, I slid her hair behind her ear, trying not to press her against her door and ravish her mouth. I had some standards.

Not many, but some.

"Let me take you out again."

She shook her head, and disappointment filled me. "I'm busy, Leif." She held up her hand as I started to argue. "I'm not saying no. I'm just saying I have lesson plans, new classes, and research. I have people to hire and countless other work things. I have a son, a new house, and boxes I still haven't unpacked. I'm doing so much, but I want to see you again, Leif. I don't know what that says about me, but I want to. I just don't know when."

Relief slammed into me so hard, that I knew I would have to worry about that later. Instead, I leaned down and brushed my lips against hers. "I think we can find some time to work with a few of those things. It doesn't have to be dinner and a movie, Brooke. It could be me helping you put up a shelf."

"Are you saying I can't put up a shelf by myself?" she asked, teasing.

"See, that's one of those tripwire questions that

women put out that I'm not going to even try to answer."

She rolled her eyes and I kissed her again.

"Go home to your kid, get some work done if that's what you're going to do, and I'll see you soon. Because there's something here, Brooke. You know there is."

I kissed her one more time and walked away before she could say no.

It was probably wrong of me, but I'd do what I had to so I could see her again.

I was just about to start my car when my phone rang and I frowned at the readout, not recognizing the number.

"Hello?"

"Leif Montgomery?" a tired voice asked, and I froze, a sense of foreboding sliding over my body.

"This is him."

"Sorry for the late call, we've been trying to get a hold of you, but we've lost some of your paperwork."

"Who is this?"

"As you're listed here as a primary contact, we're to inform you that Roger Erickson has been released on parole."

Ice slithered into my veins and I swallowed hard. "Excuse me?

"Yes, sorry it took so long to get to you. It was three weeks ago but he is out on parole."

"How can a murderer get out on parole?" I barked.

"It was all on his paperwork and sentencing. Accidental manslaughter carries a lower sentence. We can email you more information, but as you were a primary contact, we were legally required to inform you."

The man said a few other things, but I didn't listen. Instead, I tried to calm my breathing, tried to focus.

As that letter that had come to the tattoo shop crossed my mind again, and bile filled my throat.

My stepdad was out of prison.

And it seemed the past was once again slamming full force into my life.

Chapter 8

Brooke

I SHOULD HAVE KNOWN THAT ONCE I STARTED TO believe I could get the hang of things, everything would begin to crumble.

I glared at my phone as I sat in the parking lot in my car, wondering why, once again, I was getting an email that I wanted nothing to do with.

Patrice had warned me that Landon Cunning would be coming after me somehow. I just hadn't realized it would begin with passive-aggressive emails.

Brooke,

I understand starting a new job can be difficult, so why don't I handle the next afternoon meeting so you can take your time and get your ducks in a row. I wouldn't want you to overexert yourself. Don't worry. I've done this numerous times before, and I can handle it. I'm just looking out for you.

I will talk to the head adjunct. Don't you worry.

-- Landon.

I closed my eyes and tried not to snarl.

There were so many things wrong with that brief email I didn't even know where to begin.

He might as well have told me not to worry my pretty little head over it.

With any other professor, calling me Brooke would be fine. I did not want a man I didn't know who was literally coming after me using my first name. It diminished my achievements, assuming an intimacy between us that wasn't wanted in any fashion. He was purposely taking away my doctorate, my position, and my experience, so he could drop my name as if he was talking to a middle schooler.

He then tried to take over my meeting, taking it off my hands before I had even had a chance to try to prepare for it. As if I wouldn't be able to handle setting up a meeting. A meeting, by chance, that he had requested be moved up.

It was where all of us professors would meet and discuss any upcoming items we had in our department. The physics department was quite large, but my subset of it was only a few people. And Landon was one of them.

He just wanted my tenure-track job, and I wouldn't simply back down and give it to him.

The cavalier and passive aggressiveness in his email hurt my teeth. It was as if he were so sugar-sweet, butter wouldn't melt in his mouth. He would have another think coming because I didn't bow down to anyone.

Hell, I was a woman in science with a doctorate and more than one bachelor's degree. I had done it on my own, and most of it as a single mom.

I had gotten this job on my own merits, not because of who I knew. I bet he got his because of who he knew and who his father was, not because of his accomplishments.

Because, from what I saw, he didn't do anything during the day in the name of science. What *I* wasn't going to do was lie down and let him have my job.

I shot off a quick reply, letting him know in no uncertain terms that I was fine to handle the meeting, considering all that meant was that I opened the meeting and made sure people knew where it was and what time.

That was it. I didn't need to bring damn cupcakes or something. I didn't need to make a presentation.

For this first meeting, somebody just needed to book the damn room.

And contrary to what he thought, I had already done it.

So, fuck him.

"What's wrong, Mommy?" Luke asked from the backseat, and I rubbed my temples before I set my phone back in its holder, making sure it was charging.

I turned in my seat and smiled over at him. "Just a work email that made me grumpy. But I'm fine now and all here for you. You ready to run more errands?"

"I like errands!" He beamed at me, and I fell that much more in love with my son. He was just the kindest, smartest, sweetest boy ever.

I realized that was very much something that most moms said about their kids, but it was the truth.

After making sure Luke was ready to go, I settled back into my seat, pulled out of the parking lot, and headed toward our next destination.

With my job and Luke's new school, it was hard to get everything done. Thank God for grocery delivery and May. Between those two, I was able to get most of the things I needed for my house, and my shelves were never bare.

However, there were a few things that I couldn't leave to delivery or May.

We needed to pick up a few prescriptions, and I needed a new set of sheets since an entire box of linens hadn't made it onto the moving truck somehow. I still didn't know how that had happened, since we had watched it be put on the truck, but that's what happened when you moved cross-country. Things were lost. And while insurance would cover some of it, I still needed new sheets, blankets, and a few towels.

Thankfully none of Luke's things had been lost. While he was a well-adjusted kid, the move was a big thing. And losing something that he loved, even if he only would love it for the next five minutes, would've been too hard on him. I didn't want to put any more undue pressure on him.

We went to three different stores trying to find sheets that would fit my bed and were actually in stock, and I was getting grumbly by the end of it. It shouldn't be this hard to find a nice set of white sheets, but everything seemed to be out of stock or outrageously expensive.

I also needed a few things for the house, like fake plants so I wouldn't accidentally kill them, since the one from my realtor was already barely hanging on, and a tray for the kitchen. Luke was getting tired, but I had a few more items on my list.

My brain kept going to lesson plans, wanting to check my email in case Landon emailed back, and the fact that Leif hadn't texted me. Or called me. Or contacted me in any way in the past week since our date.

I let out a breath and try not to be upset about that.

He'd said that he would be out of town for a couple of days visiting family, but I had thought all his family lived in Colorado. But what did I know about him and his family? He had a job, a business he owned. He was busy.

But he hadn't texted.

I thought he would have texted.

And now I was annoyed. Because why was I worrying so much about him when I had to get my son home, had to finish my shopping, and had a thousand other things to do that had nothing to do with that Montgomery.

The same Montgomery who hadn't wanted me before but now suddenly did.

I held back a growl and went to look for a few more things that I needed for the house. I didn't even have a damn toilet brush since mine had broken as soon as I bought it. Two weeks of cleaning, and it had snapped. Now the store I went to for the matching set was out of stock. How the hell were toilet brushes out of stock? I sighed and checked out, knowing that meant we had one more store to go to.

Luke was tired, and I knew he was hungry. So was I. I didn't know the restaurants around here, and since it was lunch hour on a Saturday, there was barely any parking anywhere.

I rubbed my temples as I put everything in my trunk, and after buckling Luke in, I looked over at my son.

"I didn't plan this well. We still have to go to

another place to drop some paperwork off. I'm sorry, buddy."

Ideally all the paperwork and everything associated with moving cross-country and buying a home should have been easily organized. That was not the case for some places. Although I had all of the utilities and insurance and everything ready to go, there were still other small pieces of paperwork that had shown up out of nowhere that I needed to deal with, and I had to drop them off in person.

On a Saturday.

I still had time next week to do it if I didn't make it today, but I just wanted it to be done.

"I'm hungry, Mommy."

I looked at my kid, then leaned forward and kissed his forehead.

"Me too. I have some fish crackers if you want some, and maybe we can just head home and I will make your lunch."

"Okay. I love you, Mommy." And then he burst into tears. I rubbed my temples, knowing that I was messing things up again.

I leaned forward, unbuckled him, and held him close, rubbing his back. He was hot, tired, and had been *so* patient all day. We should have spent the day doing fun things where he could relax, and I could have mom and son bonding time. Instead, I had to be an adult and drag my kid with me. I wanted to cry right along with him.

"I'm sorry, Luke. Let's get you home, and we'll go play out in the backyard. We'll run errands another day."

"I'm sorry I'm crying. I don't know why."

Tears pricked my eyes, and I ignored the person who honked at me and wanted my spot. I was holding a crying kid who was hot, hungry, and tired.

The man flipped me off as he drove away, and I was grateful that I was holding my kid, or I would have flipped him off too.

Jerk.

"Okay, let's get you home and stop taking up space here. I could use some lunch too, kid."

"Sorry for crying. I just had a tough day."

He sounded so serious and adult-like that my eyes widened, and I just grinned. He'd probably heard that from me a time or two and had picked the phrase up. Hence why I tried not to curse around him too much since I didn't need him going to kindergarten dropping the f-bomb.

Again.

"Me too. Let's go eat something yummy."

I saw the line for a familiar fast-food restaurant behind Luke's head and figured we could sit in that line and have a greasy burger, but first I needed to buckle him in.

I did so and walked around my car and cursed under my breath as soon as I spotted it. Black dots slid over my eyes for a moment before I blinked them away, an overwhelming urge to cry along with Luke hitting me like a two-by-four.

"You have got to be kidding me."

I knelt down in front of my now flat tire and wondered how the hell that had happened so quickly. I hadn't noticed there was an issue when I'd driven earlier, but sure enough, there was a damn nail that proved to be a slow leak that hadn't stayed slow.

Luke was still in the car, and I needed to get him home, feed him, and deal with the countless other things on my list, but I couldn't because I had a damn flat tire.

In the middle of Saturday, in the middle of the parking lot, and everything that I had just bought was now piled on top of my spare.

I snarled, cursed, threatened to kick the tire, then composed myself. Then I opened the back door again. "Okay, let's get you some fish crackers because we will be a minute. Mommy has a flat tire."

Luke's eyes widened. "I didn't know you had tires."

I laughed then, mostly out of desperation. "Mommy's car has a flat tire. And hopefully, I'm going to be able to jack up this car in the parking lot."

I quickly got Luke some crackers and juice and

looked at the tire again, trying to remember the last time I'd actually changed a flat. High school? Maybe.

I opened the trunk, waving off people who wanted my spot, as I pointed to the flat tire. Nobody offered to help, which was fine because I could do this on my own, but it was quite odd that not a single person even offered.

I moved everything from the back to the seat next to Luke, and then went to get out my spare, and narrowed my eyes at it.

"Okay, you and me. We can do this. It's been years since I did this, but I can."

Or I could call AAA. Though I didn't remember if I'd changed from the California AAA to the Colorado one, and now that seemed like an oversight on my part.

I shook my head, knowing I was a strong, independent woman.

I can make this happen.

I bent over the tire in the back as a familiar voice hit my ears.

"Brooke? I thought that was you. Hell, let me help."

I nearly slammed my head on the inside of the trunk as I turned to see Leif strolling towards me, jogging slightly as he sped up.

I narrowed my eyes at him and then saw where he was coming from. Behind him, on one side of the strip, was a huge sign that spelled out Montgomery Ink Legacy.

Well. I always wanted to know where he worked, and now I did.

Because fate hated me.

"Oh. That's a coincidence," I mumbled as I tried to pull out the tire.

It fought me, and I wanted to hex it. "Seriously?"

"Here, let me help. My mom has this car, and the tires are a bitch to get out." He winced. "Sorry, Luke," he called over the back seat.

Luke crawled around and waved at him. "Hi, Leif. And it's okay. Mom already cursed."

"Tattletale," I teased, even though I was sweaty, annoyed, and felt out of sorts. I was already trying not to think about *him*. About the fact that he hadn't texted, we hadn't talked at all since our date. I was a sweaty mess, stressed out, and didn't need anybody coming in and telling me how to live my life and help me when I didn't need it. I had done this all on my own for long enough that I didn't need him to step in.

I didn't need anybody to step in.

"Here, let me help. Seriously." Leif didn't shove me out of the way, but he did bump his hip against mine, grinning.

I glowered up at him. "I've got it."

"Okay," he said, studying my face.

I realized I had snapped the words, and I hated

myself for it. I didn't know what to think, and it was all too much.

"I see you guys are out running errands. Getting a flat tire with all of that has got to be annoying." I knew he was speaking softly for Luke's benefit, trying to cut the tension, but I was so tired. Just annoyed.

"Thank you for your help, but I can handle it on my own." I sounded like a queen bitch, yet I didn't care. I just needed to get out of his parking lot and Leif didn't owe me anything.

"If you're sure."

"Now you're telling me I don't know my own mind?" I asked

His eyes widened.

"Okay. I was just trying to help out a friend." He let out a breath. "By the way, I'm sorry I haven't contacted you all week. I was out of town with my family, and like an idiot, I dropped my phone in the river." He smiled over at Luke. "Did you know that if you drop a phone in a river and it is underwater and hits a bunch of rocks, it won't work anymore?" he asked my son.

Luke's eyes widened. "One time, I dropped Mom's phone in the bathtub, and she was so mad. But then we put it in a rice bath thing, and it was fine. I think. Right, Mom?"

I grimaced, remembering the panic over him pulling my phone out of my shirt and into the tub. It was my fault for having it so close to him when he was so curious with his little grabby toddler hands.

"It all worked out. Don't worry."

"I have done that before, too, and I think I broke the phone, but I still used it for a few more months. I'm not great with phones. Oh, and Lake would've gone over the fence to say hi and tell you what was going on, but she was out of town for a presentation in New York. And I didn't want to send over anyone else to your house and be weird. I didn't borrow someone else's phone because I honestly didn't remember your number off hand because I don't even remember my own number most days. I'm sorry."

Well, that made sense, but I still just wanted to get home, feed my kid, and then go back out and run the four hundred other errands I had to do.

I barely had any time off these days as it was, and I knew this was my own doing, that this job, no matter the commitments that came with it, was my choice, but right now I felt like I kept making the wrong ones.

Was I losing too much time with my son because I wanted to further my career? Was I fighting with someone at work just to prove that I had bigger balls than he did?

I needed to stop making rash choices, but I also needed to just do things on my own. I was better when I was on my own.

"Do you want Luke to come into the shop and get

some water while you're dealing with the tire? Let me know how to help, Brooke. I want to." He stuck his hands in his pockets, and he looked so contrite, like he was trying not to scare me or anger me.

And I didn't know what was wrong with me, but I just couldn't handle it. But I needed to.

Luke needed me to handle it.

Because nobody else would.

"I got it. I had it in Paris, and I have it here."

I hadn't meant to blurt that, and when his eyes widened, I muttered under my breath.

"What?" he asked as he leaned forward.

"I'm sorry. I'm just tired." And I knew the fastest way to get home was to let him help. Because despite the strength I had in my veins, he had more muscles than I did. So I should just let him help.

It wasn't a failure, even though I felt like it was.

"I would appreciate your help with the tire. Mostly because I can't get it out of the trunk. And it's annoying me."

"Yeah, that would be annoying." He kept studying my face as if he wanted to ask more but knew he couldn't. Not in public like this, not with Luke right there, and clearly not when I acted like the bitchiest of all bitches.

"Thank you in advance," I mumbled.

He met my gaze, nodded tightly, and helped me with the tire.

In the ways of fate and men, he had the spare on in no time, while it probably would've taken me over an hour because I was out of practice and weaker than he was.

That didn't make me feel like I was helpless or anything.

"You're all good to go."

He high-fived Luke, who had stayed in the car but had stuck his head out of the window to watch.

"Be good, buddy."

"Thank you, Leif. I'll see you soon!" Luke got back in his seat, and I quickly buckled him back in, making sure he was secure, before turning to Leif.

"Thank you. I have to head home. Things are going to start melting."

Not that I had ice cream or anything in my car, but it seemed like a good excuse. I was melting as it was.

He studied my face as if he wanted to say something, but there was nothing to say.

I had to make the right choices for my son in my own life.

And I wasn't sure the man that continually went haywire on my emotions was the right choice.

"Get home safe, Brooke," Leif said, without any hint to his emotions.

Something broke inside me, but I didn't know what it was or what it meant. So I nodded my head in thanks once again, and got into my car. When I pulled out and headed home, I refused to look in the rearview mirror at him.

Because I wasn't sure what I wanted to see.

That he was still there, waiting.

Or that he was doing what he had done before and should do now: leave.

Chapter 9

Leif

I STOMPED AROUND THE FRONT YARD, SPRINKLING GRASS seed using the hand spreader. I knew Lake probably wanted me to be a little more delicate, but I wasn't in the fucking mood to care.

I wasn't in *any* mood.

I had no idea what I had done to Brooke other than be myself. I didn't know why she'd pushed me away as she had. Perhaps that was the problem. Maybe, just like before, she wanted nothing to do with me.

Oh, she might've liked that date and enjoyed that kiss, but that was it.

Because she had pushed me away.

And yet, I *had* to have done something. Brooke wasn't irrational. She was the most rational person I knew. That meant it had to be *me*.

The dumbass who kept feeling a pull to a woman who clearly didn't want me.

"Are you just going to growl at the flowers?" Nick asked from the front porch.

I flipped him off, then cringed as I looked around the neighborhood, worried that a kid had seen me do that.

"Very adult of you. I don't see any kids out, but if they're watching from the front windows, Lake will get an angry call about the big, bearded man scaring the innocent children."

"She will just have her father show up, and then the parents will swoon over Uncle Liam again." My uncle was a former model turned best-selling author. His books had been made into blockbuster movies, and most people knew his face.

Lake had been embarrassed as a kid when the parents and even some of the teenagers had swooned over her father, but now she was capitalist enough to use that to her advantage. And her father loved her enough to go with it if it meant annoying people and keeping them off Lake's lawn.

"You could just take your shirt off and do the same, you know," Nick stated, winking at me.

I scowled. "Stop hitting on me."

"You're like my brother. I would never hit on you, even though you are hot. The only other man in that house right now is Sebastian, and he's way too young for me and is practically married to that girl."

I snorted. "They do seem to be pretty serious, but he likes her, and I like Marley, too. You know there is someone else in that house. Just saying."

Nick narrowed his eyes. "I may like any gender, but I'm not going to date your cousin."

I raised a brow. "Which cousin are you talking about?" I teased.

"You are a jerk. You know I'm never going to date Lake. She's just so...*Lake*. Plus, she's taken." He practically grumbled the words.

"What do you mean by that?" Lake asked, and I cringed again as Nick stiffened and turned slowly to see Lake standing in the doorway.

"That you're taken? I thought you were dating that Zane guy." Nick raised his chin.

"His name is Zach, and yes, we are dating." She scowled before swallowing hard.

I wondered what that was about. Was it about her animosity towards Nick? Or maybe she and Zach weren't doing well. I didn't know, and it wasn't like Lake told me things when it came to dating. Oh, she might want to get all the information out of me and who I dated, but she never told me anything. Her siblings probably knew more than I did, and there was an age gap there.

But that was Lake for you. She didn't like to spill anything about herself, even though she pretended she was an open book.

"I was talking about what do you mean she's just so *Lake*. How is *Lake* an adjective?"

"You know exactly what I mean," Nick snapped before he walked past her, and she quickly darted out of the way so he wouldn't crowd her in the doorway.

She glowered at me and I raised my hands up in surrender.

"Don't glare at me. I have no idea what the hell is going on with him. And I don't know what he means by that. Other than the fact that you two do not get along, even though you guys decided to go into business with me. That's not awkward at all."

"Nick and I get along. As friends. At least, we should be. We always have been. I don't know why he gets so disgruntled whenever I'm around now."

I wasn't going to touch that with a ten-foot pole.

"Either way, thank you for reviving that part of the lawn that got screwed up with those anthills. I missed that big rain when I was out of town, and I didn't have time to worry about it myself."

"You do realize that our family has an entire landscaping division that can handle this for you." I quickly put everything away in the shed next to the house and followed Lake back inside.

"I know. I just don't like having to take up their time."

"It's not like you wouldn't pay them. They're a business. Yes, you would get the family discount, but we all decided not to do things for free for each other for things like that. Not when we didn't want to feel like we were taking advantage of anybody, even though we totally aren't."

I didn't give my family free tattoos, and I didn't get free construction work from the other arm of the family. Nor did I get free surveillance equipment from my cousins that were starting up a security firm. Yes, the discounts we got were ridiculous, and we worked at cost as much as we could because we loved each other, but we were all business people and knew that we had rules for a reason.

"I know, I know. I just like doing things myself." She shrugged, and I faltered, remembering how Brooke had said that.

"What is it with you guys? Why can't you just ask for help? I don't understand it. Yes, you can do things on your own, but it's not your responsibility to do everything on your own by pushing others away who are clearly there to help with no strings attached. It doesn't make any sense to me. You're just kicking yourself in the shin instead of actually letting someone help you."

Sebastian and Nick stared open-mouthed as Lake narrowed her gaze at me.

"I'm going to assume that has to do with somebody else, and you are not yelling at me in my own home after I allowed you to take care of the seeding even though I said I could handle it myself. You're the one who did it, and I didn't stop you. I didn't jump on your back and try to strangle you down to the ground so you wouldn't be able to do it. No, I said thank you, and I cooked dinner so that we could all eat together while discussing business. So, why don't you tell me why you're acting like such an asshole?"

I swallowed hard, then looked at Nick and Sebastian, who just shook their heads. Nick quickly took a sip of his beer while Sebastian did the same with his soda.

"Thanks for helping," I called out.

Nick snorted. "I thought I was the one digging my own grave, but it seems like you are chugging right along trying to beat me."

"You're both getting on my nerves. I'm just now remembering why I work with women-owned businesses and not with my damn cousins."

"You're not my cousin," Nick corrected Lake.

She flipped him off. "No, I'm just *Lake*. Too much of *something* for you."

Sebastian whistled between his teeth before he

went to the crockpot. "Why don't I serve everybody this delicious meal that Cousin Lake made."

"Suck up," I mumbled.

"Hell yeah," Sebastian said with a laugh. "You guys are getting her all riled up."

"Oh, so I'm a woman, therefore, I get riled up?" Lake asked, even though her eyes were filled with laughter.

"Oh good, I seem to enjoy putting my foot in my mouth like the other two. At least we're consistent."

"Write this down for when you get married to Marley. When you continually eat your own foot, dig your own grave—whatever metaphor you want to use —just shut up. Say you're sorry and move on. Things are so much easier when you just admit that you're grumbly for no reason." Lake reached out and hugged Sebastian, and it surprised me that Sebastian was so much taller than her.

He was a man, no longer a kid, easily above six foot like the rest of us, and broadening out with muscle nearly every day.

There was a reason he was here with us for this business meeting. He might not have bought into the company yet, but he would. This was what he wanted with his life, and we wanted him here with us.

We went over financials and projections and made sure that our business was where it needed to be. Sebastian had input as well. He might not be a voting member yet, but we trusted him. And he was a brilliant kid.

It was the fact that he *wasn't* a kid anymore that was startling to me. Many of my cousins were now old enough to drink and start new lives. Lake and I were no longer the only Montgomery adult kids.

It was an odd transition in our lives, but I was grateful for it. No more dirty diapers, daycare, and afterschool plays. At least not until our generation started having kids.

It was such an odd thought, considering it had made up my entire life since I had joined the family, but I liked it.

Of course, that just reminded me of who lived next door.

A woman who might not have to deal with dirty diapers anymore, but she still had to deal with daycare and perhaps afterschool plays and meetings.

Things she could do all on her own because God forbid she ask for help. Or at least take help if it was offered without any strings.

"Where's your head at?" Lake asked, pointing at me with her fork.

I looked over at her and shrugged. "Probably where it shouldn't be."

"At least you're honest," she said with a laugh. "Does it have anything to do with the fact that you haven't told me how your date went with my neighbor other than *okay*?"

"It probably has more to do with him seeing her in the parking lot today and coming back inside like a lion with a thorn in his paw."

"Shut up, Nick," I growled.

"I don't believe I will." Nick turned to Lake and Sebastian and grinned. "I don't know what happened, but he saw her out there and decided to practically run to her like a kid seeing candy in the window. And then he came back in grumbling and was an asshole. He hasn't stopped being one since."

"That's it. Our friendship is over." I narrowed my eyes at my best friend.

"If that's all it took for you to lose me as a friend, I'm surprised we lasted this long." Nick laughed. "Honestly, what happened?"

"She had a flat tire and practically ripped my face off for offering to help. I don't know what I did wrong, but in the end, she let me help because it was the easiest way for me to get out of her face. Apparently."

"Oh, Leif." The sound of resignation in Lake's voice made me turn.

"What did I do?"

"Let me guess, she was out running errands, was tired, and she had a flat tire. Did you just show up and offer to help without her asking?"

"Of course I did. Even if we hadn't gone on a date,

I consider her a friend. I'd do the same for someone who *could* be my friend. Or a stranger who needed help. She literally couldn't get the nuts off the tire. I wasn't telling her she couldn't do it, but she *literally* couldn't. I just don't know why she had to treat me like that."

Lake shook her head. "Of course, you do. She was embarrassed. And she's been a single mom for Luke's entire life. She has no real friends or family out here, although we will change the friends part. She's been alone and independent, doing things by herself for long enough that anybody coming into her space seems like a threat. You may not get it, but as a woman? I one hundred percent get it. I'm not saying that she is completely in the right here. But I see where she's coming from and why she reacted the way she did. It's not your fault, it's not her fault, but it still is your fault," she said, cringing.

"I hate the fact that I understood that," I grumbled.

"Hold on, I need to start taking notes," Sebastian said as he pulled out his phone.

Nick looked over Sebastian's shoulder and shrugged. "Forward that to me."

I looked at all three of them, knowing they were trying to lighten the mood, and I shook my head. "I hate that I screwed things up."

"Are you sure you screwed things up? Or perhaps

you two just need to talk when you're not stressed out in a parking lot." Lake squeezed my hand.

I sighed. "I think you need to start writing a book with some of our cousins so you can explain to us idiots how women work."

"I would read it," Sebastian put in.

"I'm fine," Nick added, and Lake laughed.

"Sure you are, honey. Whatever you say."

"Don't call me honey," he growled.

"Whatever, babycakes."

"Do you call Zach those names?" Nick asked.

"I call Zach whatever he wants me to," she singsonged and went to clear off the table. Sebastian immediately began to help her as Nick went to start the dishes.

"Leif, can you go take a look at the hose out back? I think it might be melded to the house because I left it connected too long. Don't tell Dad."

I laughed and did as she asked, knowing that she could do that on her own, but she was asking for my help—probably because she knew I was stressed out over the whole situation with Brooke.

I walked out to the backyard, undid the hose from the wall, and made a note to tell Lake to get a new one.

A soft sound hit my ears, and I turned to see Brooke pacing in the backyard, a glass of wine in her hand. She stared up at the sky, then back down at the ground.

It was late enough that Luke might be in bed, but I didn't know the nighttime routine of a five-year-old. I just knew that looking at Brooke under the moonlight did things to me I didn't want to name.

I walked towards the low gate in between the two homes and swallowed hard. I didn't want to startle her, so I cleared my throat as I walked. She whirled around, sloshing wine out of the glass. I winced.

"I'm sorry. I didn't mean to scare you."

Brooke looked at me then and gave a hollow laugh before she took a sip of her wine. "I was off thinking about nothing, not paying attention to my surroundings." She pulled her phone out of her pocket, checked the readout, and slid it away. "I have video alerts in Luke's room. So if he moves a certain way, I'll get a ping. Got to love technology, right? I don't think they had these things when I was a kid. At least not as motion sensitive."

"I don't even think my mom would've done something like that if the technology did exist when I was five. I know Sierra did for the twins, though."

Brooke smiled softly. "I'm glad that you have her. She was nice at the store."

"She's the best." We were silent for so long that I was afraid she would walk inside and leave my life forever, but that sounded so dramatic that I pushed the thought away. I was an adult. I could use my words. I should just fucking say what was on my mind. "What did you mean about Paris before? In the parking lot?"

She froze and studied my face. I was so afraid she wasn't going to say anything, that she would brush it off and walk away. But Paris lay between us. It always had, and it always would, no matter what we did at this moment. I needed to know what she meant, and I needed to know why. Because if I didn't, I knew that nothing would come from today or tomorrow. And part of me didn't want that, but part of me was so scared of what she might say, I didn't even know what to think.

She let out a sigh. "I came back to Colorado, you know."

I froze. Because she couldn't be saying what I thought she was.

Brooke hadn't come back to Colorado. I knew that as fact. It was the whole basis for having my heart ripped open all those years ago. She hadn't come back to Colorado to see me after Paris. That had to be the truth.

"What?"

Brooke narrowed her gaze. "You know this. You had to have known this."

"No, I don't. What the hell are you talking about?"

"I came back to Colorado. I didn't go directly to California. I came here."

The *for you* was left unsaid, but I heard it none-theless.

"Then why didn't you meet me at Taboo?"

Because that was what the plan had been. We'd had hot and heavy nights in Paris, and I had fallen in love with the girl when I shouldn't have. We had both been young, carefree, and about to start radically different lives. I shouldn't have fallen in love with her, but I had. And she had told me she had as well. We were supposed to meet at Taboo on a certain day, at a certain time, but she had never shown.

So when I saw her at Taboo that morning years later, even after knowing she had moved back, it was like a blast from the past. I hadn't been able to stay away.

That was why I had kissed her.

And that was why I still wanted to kiss her.

She met my gaze. "I went to Taboo. On the second. I stood there and waited, acting as if my heart wasn't breaking because you didn't come." Her eyes were wet with the sheen of tears, but I stood there, shaking my head before I laughed.

I couldn't help but laugh.

"Are you laughing right now? I waited for you, Leif. And you never showed."

"I was there, you know. Every day as soon as I got back. I was there on April fourth. Just like we planned. And then I was there on the fifth. The sixth. I was there every day for a week, but you never came. I even told Hailey and the others what you looked like so they could call me and I could show up. You never showed. But it seems like I was days late."

"Are you kidding me? No, it was the second."

I leaned over the fence and cupped her face. "How did we miss out on so much because of a broken, bittersweet promise? How did I miss you for so long because we had the date wrong?"

She shook her head, her eyes wide. "Are you serious right now?"

"Apparently."

"But if I had met you there, Leif, I still would've had to go to California. At least for the year before I came back for undergraduate. And then, I needed to go to California again to go to graduate school and meet Henry. Because I needed to have Luke. It just doesn't make any sense."

"Damn it," I whispered before I leaned over and pressed my forehead to hers. "Maybe we needed to walk past one another and not realize that we had been wrong. But now we're back. So, what happens next?"

In answer, I leaned forward again and brushed my lips to hers.

And thankfully, she kissed me back.

I might have a few answers from the past and far more questions for the future, but at least I had this.

This moment. For now.

Chapter 10

Brooke

The last of the incoming graduate students left my office, and I sighed as I leaned back in my chair, grateful that the door was closed.

I had known this job would be difficult, as I hadn't had an easy time of it as a graduate student myself. So being on the other side of the desk would be a different yet just as complicated experience.

I had once been the student vying for a seat with my favorite professor. There were only so many graduate students a professor could handle during a year. Not only did they have to deal with funding since we were providing their stipend, even through the school, but we also had to deal with time, desk space, and research opportunities.

I could handle three to five graduate students, and I knew that I would be getting them. I just had to try for the ones that I wanted. The large pool of incoming first-years had ideas of their own and knew where they wanted to go. Because I was the new professor, starting from the ground up, some students were eager to get a foothold. Others wanted to go to someone who had been here for years and would be able to fit into a place where there wouldn't be the extra hurdles of starting from scratch and making sure the academic world knew that you existed.

While I had connections to my previous schools and other professors and postdocs that I had worked with in the past, I was still a relative unknown. And that meant luring students to my cause wasn't easy. We had the space, and the funds, but finding the perfect student for my research wasn't an easy task.

Each student had to meet with at least five professors, and many of them met with more than that. Many students came in knowing what kind of research they wanted to do. Others had no idea, only that they wanted a higher education.

My job was to find students that worked with the personalities of Randall, Jennifer, and Hannah. They were already working for me, Randall was teaching a class for undergraduates, Jennifer was working on her thesis, at least the initial preparations for it, and Hannah was still taking classes as a second-year grad student. I wanted the full five first-year grads, I didn't think I was going to be able to get them, but three to five would be a great start to my career here and the building blocks needed for my students to thrive.

And that meant research, schmoozing, and fighting other professors for the students. Not that we actually *fought* for them. At least not so far. If anything, everybody looked like they were ready to find the students that worked for them and make sure that every student found a match.

This was in addition to the undergraduate class I was teaching, the graduate class I would be teaching next semester that I still needed to prepare for, my own research, and the day-to-day life of a professor at a university.

Sometimes I thought my life would have been easier if I had gone into industry, rather than academics, but I had taken this route for a reason. I enjoyed the connections, the research, and helping the new generation, even though sometimes I felt like I was *still* that young generation.

But it meant long nights, and my son having the patience of a saint. It didn't help that right now a feeling of inadequacy filled me.

It was after five, and I knew I would be missing dinner tonight, as meetings were planned in advance, but I still hated that May was feeding my son, cooking for him, and if I didn't get home early enough, would end up tucking him in.

This only happened once or twice a month, and I wouldn't allow for it to happen more frequently. Patrice at least understood, and I hoped the other professors would as well.

People would just have to find a way to make it work, because I needed to be there for my son like I always had, and always would be.

It was just in these moments that the little voice in my head kept telling me that I was a horrible mother.

I went through the last of my emails and made sure I was ready to go. I stood up, looking up at the door, expecting to see Randall. He was teaching an evening course, something he actually enjoyed doing because he preferred to sleep in. It was a perfect pairing since I tended to wake up early to get my day going.

But it wasn't my postdoc in my doorway. No, it was the person I least wanted to see. I rolled my shoulders back and told myself to ignore the unsettled feeling in my stomach.

"Hello there, Dr. Cunning, what can I do for you?"

"Dr. *Adler*," he said, putting an odd emphasis on my name. I knew he did that on purpose, like he wanted to call me Brooke.

He really was an asshole. I was trying not to put my

preconceived notions on him, but it was hard not to when he kept acting like the asshole that he was.

He wanted my job, didn't get it, and his apparent plan was to ruin my enjoyment of it.

That wasn't going to happen. I was in a tenure-track position, and I was not going to lose my job. There was another opening coming up in a year or two, and it was all but in writing that Landon would get it. He had been second runner-up for my job, and the person who had been runner-up had taken a job at Harvard.

There was literally no reason for Landon to do this, other than he didn't want to wait until he could get a job that was handpicked for him.

It made no sense to me other than he didn't like to lose, and he wasn't used to hearing the word no.

He was going to have to get used to it because I wasn't having any of his nonsense.

"I'm just heading home. Is there anything that you needed?"

I knew better than to ask questions like that. I should've asked why he was here. But no, I had to be the helper.

I was usually better than that, but he always rattled me, and it threw me off my game. I was off my game for many things, but I wasn't going to think about that right then.

"I just wanted to see how the recruitment was

going. I know it can be difficult for a new teacher. One who doesn't really have the experience that others have when it comes to bringing others to their team. I'm here if you need any advice. Or if you'd like me to speak to a few of the other professors for you. That way I can grease the wheels a bit to make sure you get who you need. I would hate for you to start the year without the right number of students. I mean, what could happen if you didn't have the research and papers that you needed in order to qualify for your next position?"

I nearly closed my eyes and told myself that beating a man senseless wasn't going to help anyone.

It might make me feel better, though.

"I have it all handled. Thank you for looking out for me. I truly appreciate it."

The sickly sweet tone escaping my lips was a little much for me, but he didn't seem to mind. Instead, something flared in his eyes, something I didn't quite recognize, and I wasn't sure I wanted to. I was tired and wanted to go home to my son, and this jerk just wouldn't go away.

And I knew if I told him to leave me alone, to stop bothering me, to walk away, he would go to all his little professor friends and say that I was a nuisance. I was the one who couldn't handle it and was bothering him. Because, after all, he was just trying to help a fellow teacher, someone new. They wouldn't hear the undertones. They wouldn't see exactly what he was doing.

So I would just have to handle this myself. Like I always did. I had dealt with people like him before, and I would again in the future. I just had to get through this one thing, and I wouldn't let Landon and his ilk bother me.

"If you're sure." He sneered as he said it, and I raised my chin.

"I'm sure. Have a good night then."

He narrowed his gaze. "Brooke."

I sighed as he closed the door behind him, and I wished there was a way to fix this. But there wouldn't be. Landon didn't want to be my friend, there was no way I could change how he felt about me. He wanted my job. He didn't think I was qualified, and he was going to do whatever he could to ensure that I was uncomfortable and unhappy.

I wasn't going to let him have that power over me.

I was stronger than that.

At least, that's what I was telling myself.

I packed my things and headed to the lab. Randall was working, his head bowed over his laptop and data.

"Everything okay?" I asked my postdoc.

He looked up, his eyes wide. Then he shook his head, that numb glaze over his eyes fading away. "Oh, I'm good. Sorry, I was deep in it, and didn't hear you come up."

I smiled. "Honestly, that's what I like to hear."

He smiled back at me. "Sounds like a good day to me. Say hi to Luke for me. That kid is pretty awesome."

I had brought Luke in a couple of days prior so he could see my office, and he had met my team. I was grateful that so far my team liked Luke. Honestly, it was easy when it came to my son. He bowled everybody over no matter who they were, or how they felt about kids. I was never going to ask one of them to babysit or watch Luke. There were boundaries, and I wasn't going to encroach. But I also wanted Luke to feel comfortable wherever I was at.

"I will tell him. And I agree. He is pretty awesome." I went over a few more things with Randall and promised I would see him after the weekend. Thankfully, we had a three-day weekend, though I knew some people would be coming onto campus to work. I would be doing mine from home, just going over papers and assignments. Randall might come in, but the rest of my team wouldn't. I trusted my team to get things done, and they knew that they could come to me with anything.

Landon was still in his office, his feet on the desk, laughing loudly over the phone as he talked with someone, and I moved quickly, hoping he didn't see me. I did not want to have to go head-to-head with him again. I just wanted to see my kid and not feel like an absolute failure because it was getting late.

Yes, he would be able to stay up a little bit later tonight because he didn't have school in the morning, but I also just missed my kid.

My schedule was a lot more flexible, and I had to keep that in mind. That was why we moved to Colorado, why I had left Caltech. At least, that was one of the reasons.

I just had to remember that I had been doing this on my own in some fashion since before Luke was born, and that wasn't going to change anytime soon. I could do this.

I had to.

I pulled into my garage, exhausted, anxious to see my boy.

I grabbed my things from my passenger seat and closed the garage door behind me, walking into the house to the smell of some form of stir-fry, the sound of my kid laughing, and May giggling.

"I told you I was going to get you!" May called out, her voice a little deeper with a fake growl.

I grinned as Luke giggled and May attacked him, the tickle monster in full force. Luke kicked his legs up in the air, and May dug her fingers into his stomach, albeit gently.

"I see that Luke has succumbed to the tickle

monster again. I told him he had to be faster. We'll just have to practice."

"Mommy!" Luke called out, the sound music to my ears. In fact, it was so perfect that tears sprung to my eyes, and I swallowed hard, going down to my knees as I opened my arms. Luke slammed into me, wrapping his arms around my shoulders, as May gave me a sloppy smile.

"I missed you, buddy," I whispered, kissing Luke's cheek.

He was warm and smelled of little boy, plus sugar, and whatever he'd eaten for dinner. It was pre-bath time, but I was home, which meant I could have fun with bath time.

It was these moments I treasured.

Not those when I felt inadequate, and that I was failing.

"I missed you too, Mommy." He pulled away and spun in a circle. "May beat me in wrestling, but I'll get her. Don't worry."

I looked over at May, who rolled her eyes. "He may think he can overpower me, but he doesn't know the strength in these wee arms." May flexed her arms, and Luke clapped and shook his little butt.

The smile on my face grew. "You're probably stronger than me. Just saying."

May winked. "There is no probably about it. I'm swole."

I burst out laughing as May grinned and Luke looked at us in confusion, before he joined in laughing.

I would explain that word later.

"Thank you for staying late tonight. I appreciate it."

"No problem. It's part of the perks. I made extra dinner for you. So all you have to do is heat it up. We had honey garlic chicken with green beans and broccoli."

"Really?" I asked, surprised. I looked over at my kid. "That sounds yummy."

"It was so good. And May helped me cook."

I narrowed my gaze. "So you did the cooking?" I asked.

"May was my sous chef."

"You're going to have to teach me that recipe," I said seriously.

"No problem. I actually wrote it all down for you, and was going to email it as well. I figured if it gets us to our vegetables, it's a win."

I nodded, grateful. "We like vegetables over here," I said, as I wrapped my arms around Luke again.

"I guess chocolate for tomorrow since we had vegetables today," Luke said quickly, darting his gaze from me.

I sighed, and then attacked his belly, making him giggle. "Only if you defeat tickle monster's boss."

May laughed and shook her head as Luke giggled, and I moved quickly out of the way of a flying shoe.

"Okay buddy, let's calm you down. I'm giggling at this point," I said with a laugh.

I just liked that I was in a better mood. I was happier.

Because I was here with my kid. Maybe I did do the right thing, moving him out here and changing his life completely.

After our Luke attack, we got May all packed up and headed towards the door.

"Seriously, thank you."

"You don't have to thank me for being part of your life. I love what I do. I love that you trust me enough with Luke. He is the brightest and best little boy. And I'm honored that I get to be part of this journey. I know it's not easy for you to not be here at all times of day, but I'm here. I promise. I'm not taking over anything. I'm just here to help when I can."

Once again, tears pricked my eyes, and I smiled at the other woman.

"I guess we make a pretty good team."

"Yes, we do."

The doorbell rang right as I was walking May out, and I blinked. I looked over at her. "Expecting someone?

"Well, it's six o'clock on a Thursday evening, so no," May said with a laugh.

I looked through the peephole and froze, swallowing hard. "Oh."

May's eyes filled with interest, a grin on her face.

"That sounds like a good 'oh,' I hope."

I sighed, and then steeled myself, opening the door. "Hi, Leif. I didn't know you were coming by."

May nearly dropped her bag and looked between us. "Leif?"

An odd sensation filled me. They *knew* each other. From the way the two of them were staring at one another, surprise on their faces, something happened that I wasn't sure I wanted to know about.

My stomach tightened but I forced myself to smile. "I see the two of you know each other."

Leif gave me a soft smile that actually reached his eyes. He didn't even have the grace to look guilty, even though I wasn't sure what he had to be guilty about.

"May. It's good to see you again." He turned to me. I tried not to stare at him. It was hard to do so since I always wanted to look at him.

"Brooke, May is that blind date I told you about. The one that Lake set me up with? A small world."

"Oh," I said, my eyes wide, pieces coming together slowly as I relaxed marginally.

"He told you about the date?" May asked, nervousness in her tone. "It was literally just dinner. Leif is a nice guy, and I adore Lake. But wow. The two of you? I totally have questions."

I turned to my nanny, then Leif, and swallowed hard. "No, I thought the world was small when it came to Montgomerys, I didn't realize it was also small concerning your friends and past lives," I said dryly.

"A single blind date, but it was a good dinner." Leif winked at May, who just rolled her eyes, the tension easing between all of us thankfully.

"Dinner was good. But sadly, no sparks." May shrugged. "I'm looking for sparks. I'm not great at it, but I'm looking."

I smiled then. "I wasn't looking for sparks."

Left unsaid was that the sparks came anyway. May grinned at me as Leif's eyes darkened...and I realized we were on the same wavelength.

Oops. I might as well have shouted that last part, instead of keeping it to myself. Because they both had heard it anyway.

"Anyway, I have to go," May said, before practically running out of the house to her car.

Leif looked back at her, then at me. That was when I noticed the pink box in his hands.

"I didn't know you were coming by." I hadn't meant to sound so accusatory, but Leif just shrugged.

"I stopped by at Lake's to drop off paperwork, I figured I would drop off the cupcakes that I brought for you. And Luke of course, but I'm not going to mention them to him until you give me the okay."

At the sound of his deep voice, Luke came running in.

"Leif!" Luke said, as he practically ran towards the man. Leif handed me the box of cupcakes, then went to his knees and hugged Luke. Then he got up and spun Luke around on the porch as Luke laughed and talked Leif's head off.

I stood there, wondering how on earth this had happened.

I did not date. *Ever.* And I had told myself when I did start dating, I would not include Luke. That was the rule. Luke could not get attached to anyone.

Except for the fact that the two of them had met before I had a chance to keep them apart.

And with the way that Leif was talking to Luke as if the two of them were best friends, I knew there was no doing that now.

It wasn't only going to be *my* heart that broke when things fizzled out.

I had to be better. Had to not think about the worst-case scenarios. Even if it was the only thing I could think of.

"Leif brought cupcakes," I said, knowing that this much sugar tonight would be a bad idea, but then again, I was getting good at bad ideas.

"Cupcakes?" Luke looked up at Leif, his eyes wide. "Really? Thank you!"

"I did and you're welcome." Leif grinned down at my son and my heart did a little twisty thing.

Luke scrambled down and came up to me. "Can I have one?" he asked, his eyes wide. "Please?"

"Of course, you can. I wouldn't have mentioned them if you couldn't." I leaned down and kissed the top of his head. "Can you be really careful and bring the box into the kitchen? And if Leif has time, he can have some with us."

I met Leif's gaze. He smiled softly, the understanding there worrying me.

"I would love to. I have all the time in the world."

Luke cheered, and then carefully walked the pink box into the kitchen, out of sight, as I stood there in front of Leif, shaking my head.

"Apparently you not only dated my nanny, but you have also made my son fall in love with you. I'm a little worried."

"You know when you said your nanny's name was May, it honestly didn't click that it might be the same person. It should have, because that's our connection it seems, but it didn't." He leaned forward and cupped my cheek. "I didn't even kiss her, Brooke. I promise. There's been no one but you."

I swallowed hard, that familiar tight sensation shocking me. "Same here."

"You didn't kiss May?"

That twinkle in his eyes made me smile. "I didn't. She is my nanny, after all."

"I hear there are books that encourage that notion."

"Sadly, I'm not living in a romance book with May. But she is the best nanny ever. So I'm glad that you two ended on good terms."

"There was nothing to end. Just a good dinner, and I got to meet Lake's boyfriend."

My eyes widened. "You got to meet Zach? I haven't got to meet him even though I hear all about him."

"I don't hear much about him, so you should totally tell me everything, that way I can act like the big brother."

I laughed, shaking my head. "I thought she was your cousin."

"Same difference." Then he leaned down and brushed his lips up against mine. I let out a shuddering moan, even though I tried to hold it back. I parted my lips ever so slightly to slide my tongue along his.

He let out a moan then pulled away, visibly shaken. Since I was the exact same, I swallowed hard.

"Okay, enough of that, especially with your kid in the next room."

I blushed. "Thank you for that. Okay, let's go have cupcakes."

"Cupcakes sound wonderful. Thank you for inviting me, Brooke."

It's scary how his words nearly knocked me off my feet. I swallowed hard, wondering what the hell I was doing.

"Thank you for bringing them. And just, well, thank you."

Then I moved to the kitchen, knowing he was following me.

I had no idea what I was doing. And yet, it seemed like once again I couldn't stop doing it.

Chapter 11

Leif

Today was all about skulls and roses. I grinned as I worked on the final shading on the current skull with the rose crown.

"How is it looking?" Christy asked, and I kept silent, my focus on my work, not answering.

"You know he's not going to answer you. Not when you're nearing the end. You're just going to have to wait and be surprised," Nick said from his station.

Christy let out a breath but kept perfectly still, like she had been the entire session.

She was a trooper, didn't complain about pain, didn't bleed, and as this was her fourth tattoo with me, she knew the ins and outs of aftercare and actually listened to my instructions.

By the time I was finished and had washed off excess ink and plasma, I knew Christy was champing at the bit to get a look.

"Okay, are you ready?" I asked.

She smiled up at me. "I've been ready since you took away the mirror and didn't let me watch the progress anymore. You're a mean one, Leif Montgomery."

"I really am. The meanest. Now, take a look and tell me what you think."

My stomach twisted at that thought, waiting to see her reaction. We had gone over the sketch and incorporated the designs from her childhood. Each flower, whether blooming or wilted, was significant to her in the memories she had chosen to ink on her skin. This one piece was a small part of the growing art on her thigh. We wanted it to look like a forest that the viewer would travel through and find parts of her.

Her heart, her memories, her past, and her future.

This was the art that I loved to do most. Yes, I painted, molded clay, sketched with charcoal, among other things, and I sold what I could, and I enjoyed it.

Working with somebody else to create something that was a permanent fixture on their bodies meant something special to me. Something that couldn't be replicated on paper because the person wearing it added their own layer of…magic.

"Leif…" She let out a breath. "It looks so real. Like it's 3D and coming out of my skin. I cannot believe this is what we worked on. It's even better than I could've imagined. And I know your work, so I was already imagining perfection."

Christy, the woman who didn't cry, didn't show any emotion when it came to the pain of getting a tattoo, choked up as she spoke, and I swallowed hard.

"Glad to see it meets your approval," I said with a wink, trying to cut the tension. Christy wouldn't like anyone else knowing she cried like a human being. She liked to be stoic, sarcastic, a little bitter. She showed the world what she wanted them to see. So I was going to do my best to make sure the world saw that.

Even if it made me grin and fill with pride at the thought that she had broken just a little bit of that shell of hers because of my work.

"It more than meets my approval. It's utterly fantastic. Seriously. Thank you. I cannot wait to see what it looks like when I'm not so swollen, and it's healed. Now I'm thinking about the next piece we're going to do." She grinned up at me as I shook my head, smiling back at her.

"We can get you on the schedule. But let's make sure this heals first."

She rolled her eyes as she sat back down on my

bench and I finished cleaning her up and setting her up with the Saniderm. Technology had changed a lot in the last few years, and with this and the special creams that we had, it would heal quickly.

My dad still marveled at how things had changed since he had started in this business; considering how much had changed in the years I had been doing it, I could only imagine.

"You have a lifetime canvas with me," Christy said with a laugh. "Of course, at one point we may run out of skin, so I'm just going to have to bring in friends."

"Bring in as many as you can," Nick said. "You know us, we're just trying to make a living here. We don't want to end up doing tattoos on the street in exchange for bread." He winked as he said it, and though Christy laughed, sometimes I was still afraid that's what we would end up doing.

We still had a full roster, with some time for walk-ins, but we were still new. We had made it past the first year with all the issues that had crept up, but unless we were here for at least three years, I didn't think I would ever be completely comfortable.

Of course, if you asked Nick or anyone on my team, they would tell me I would never relax fully when it came to comparing this place to the other two locations.

I needed to make my family proud.

I couldn't be the one to screw it all up.

We booked Christy for six months out, and as she left, she waved and said that she would actually be back sooner, with a friend.

I relaxed, letting out a breath as Leo walked in, a brow raised.

"Why do you look as if you want to throw up?" he asked as Nick chuckled under his breath.

"I'm glad you're the one who said it instead of me."

"I'm fine," I said, knowing I was lying. I went to clean up my station as Nick worked on the large body-builder next to me.

"What's up?" Leo asked, setting his sketchpad in his own station.

"Just thinking of worst-case scenarios. You know me," I said as casually as possible.

"You know, as a business owner myself, it's our job to think about worst-case scenarios, but I hope you do know how to relax."

I looked over at our other client, a large man not even looking up at us. Considering Nick was doing a piece on his back, it made sense.

"See, listen to Freddie here. He has owned his lawn and sprinkler maintenance company for twenty years. He knows what he's doing."

"Oh yeah?" I asked, honestly interested.

"Hell yeah. I've even worked with your family before," Freddie added as he turned his head slightly without moving the rest of his body, so that way he didn't screw up the tattoo. "You Montgomerys have great businesses, so it's all in the blood when it comes to you. I like it. Whenever they need extra help with sprinkler systems, they call my company. Your family does more of the planting and growing and designing, so I like it when they call on my business. Keeps everything local, and somewhat small, even though you guys are practically a corporation at this point."

I snorted, shaking my head. "Small world."

"Not when it comes to the Montgomerys," Nick grumbled, and I had to wonder what that was about. Because there was something there I couldn't quite figure out, only I wasn't about to grill my best friend in front of Leo and Freddie.

"It is true, I'm constantly bumping into one of you guys," Leo teased.

I narrowed my gaze at the other man. I liked him; he was a hard worker, a brilliant artist, and was just out of apprenticeship. "We're not that bad."

"Yes, you are. But you're good people, and you take care of those who work with you," Freddie said.

"We try," I said, looking over at Leo who shrugged.

Freddie leaned forward. "I'm taken care of, and if you're anything like your old man, you will take care of me in this business for decades."

"That's what I like to hear." Leo winked, then went back to his work as if he hadn't put more pressure on my shoulders. No, that wasn't his fault. I was the one putting pressure on my own shoulders, and I had to get used to that. I had to stop comparing myself to my father.

It just wasn't easy when my dad was the best guy I knew, and damn good at his job. I didn't want to be the one who tarnished the family name by getting their business shut down for not being able to pay the bills. Not that we were anywhere close to that, but those worst-case scenarios wouldn't go away in my head. No matter how hard I tried. And no matter how hard Nick tried to get me out of my own head.

A few more clients walked in, as did the rest of our team, and I went back to work on a few drawings. By the end of the day, I'd done two small tattoo walk-ins and prepped for my bigger project the next day. I purposely left my afternoon off to work on business things with Lake if she came in, and for any walk-ins and future drawings.

After lunch I took some charcoal to canvas, let out my feelings, just trying to see what came to mind. I would sell it to a local gallery if I felt it was worth it, so that way today didn't end up completely useless.

What the hell was wrong with me? I did good work, had made three clients very happy, and had consulted with my team on numerous projects.

I wasn't wasting my day just because I wasn't bent over a table, working until my eyes bled. I was tired of sounding whiny, so I wasn't going to be. I was better than that.

Damn it.

My phone buzzed. I looked down at it, hoping it was Brooke, but I knew it wasn't going to be her. She said she was in meetings all day, and then was going to try to rush home so she could spend time with her son. She told me point-blank that fitting a relationship into her life right now wasn't going to work, yet we were still kind of trying. Maybe I need to try harder. I brought cupcakes for her, but that wasn't enough. She had more on her plate than anyone I knew, so I needed to do more.

Only I wasn't quite sure how to do that.

One minute I was worried about work, now suddenly I was trying to woo and help a single mom. That wasn't exactly what I thought I'd be doing with my day, and yet I didn't want anything else.

My phone buzzed again, and I frowned, not recognizing the number.

Most of my team had left, Leo out front working on a sketch with Nick.

I picked up the phone, answering it even though I usually let unknown numbers go to voicemail.

"Hello."

"Boy. Good to hear that voice."

Chills skittered up my spine and I froze, that

familiar voice slamming into me like a thousand shards of pain and memory that would never fade away.

"Roger."

Nick's head shot up at that. He set his notebook next to Leo, leaving the other man behind. Nick hovered over me; his arms folded over his chest as he glared at the phone.

I ignored him, as well as Leo's curious stare. I tried my best not to sound like an asshole. If I reacted in any way other than nonchalance, Roger would win. It had been that way when I was a kid, and nothing had changed since the other man had gotten out of prison. Not with the way Roger had sneered the word *boy*.

"You should call me dad. You know I like it when you call me dad."

I held back my revulsion as Nick took the phone out of my hand and set it on speaker. He gestured toward Leo, who gave us a look and went back to the office, closing the door and giving us a semblance of privacy.

I had a good team, and I was grateful. Right then I just wanted to hang up the phone and be alone.

"I hear you're out of prison. Not quite sure why you're calling me."

"I just wanted to say hi. It's been a long time, Leif."

Not long enough.

"Well, you did that. Goodbye, Roger."

"Don't hang up on me. You're not going to like it."

I hung up on him, knowing the other man had no power over me. He might have when I was a kid, but I was an adult now, and Roger had nothing to do with me.

He was my past and was no part of my present or future.

Then why did just the sound of his voice bring me back to his beatings, to the way that he would grip my shoulder, and force me to listen as he told me how worthless I was?

"He sounds like an asshole," Nick said casually, though there was nothing casual about his voice.

"He is. I don't know what he wants, but I'm pretty sure that threat performance was from him."

Nick nodded, his gaze going dark. "That note? Figured as much. You talk to your parents about it?"

I shook my head. "Roger has nothing to do with them. I don't want to worry them."

Nick met my gaze and narrowed his eyes. "You're keeping secrets. It's going to bite you in the ass."

"Maybe. But the other man can't do anything to me. And all he has done so far is call. And maybe sent that note. Hell, I just don't want my parents to worry."

"I think you're making a mistake, but it's yours to make. I'm here if you need me. Okay?"

Bile rose in my throat, but I nodded tightly as my best friend patted my shoulder in a way that reminded me of Roger. I quickly squashed that thought. I'd been hugged, touched, and roughed around before. I hadn't thought of Roger then. My real father had never hurt me, never laid a hand on me in anger. I even played football and soccer in high school and dealt with it easily.

I wouldn't flinch away when my best friend touched me in comfort.

Leo walked out then, looking between us. "The door isn't that thick, so I heard most of that, I'm sorry. I wanted to blast music or something because then you'd know I know."

I cursed under my breath. "My stepdad's out of prison. Or I should just call him my birth mom's boyfriend. Technically, she never married him."

"I'm sorry. Is there anything we can do?" Leo asked.

I shook my head. "Just ignore him. He has my phone number for some reason, and while that worries me, and I think he has the address to this place, he's an old man now. He can't hurt us." I didn't know if I was saying that more for them or myself. Probably both. "It's probably a good idea to make sure that we keep the place locked-up tight, make sure the security is on."

"We always do but will be doubly sure. You should tell your parents," Nick said again.

I sighed. "I don't want to bother them."

Leo looked between us but didn't say anything. Instead, we went back to work, and after a few moments of pretending to go back to the charcoal, I picked up my phone. I wondered if I was making mistake.

Me: *How did the day go?*

Brooke: *Long, I'm glad I'm home. How are you?*

I almost told her everything. Right then and there, I almost texted it all to her. She did not need that on her shoulders. She didn't need anything else on her plate.

Me: *I got to play with art and met some interesting people. So, I guess it's a good day.*

Brooke: *You have to show me some of your pieces. That way I can gear up if I'm ever ready for a tattoo.*

The thought of being the one to put art on her skin made me swallow hard. I wanted to be the one to do that, nobody else. Maybe that made me a territorial jerk, but I was what I was.

Me: *You say the word and I'm there.*

Brooke: *I would never trust anyone else.*

My heart thumped loudly, those words doing more to me than I ever thought possible.

Me: *What do you say to dinner tomorrow?*

Brooke: *I say yes. I think I need it.*

She was so quick to say that, so I knew it was true. I bit my lip and quickly made plans with her, wondering if I was making mistake.

Then again, I couldn't be. Not when it came to

Brooke. Because I had made the mistake earlier, I wasn't going to do it again.

Despite my own misgivings, my own issues, I was falling for Brooke.

Too hard. Too fast.

And yet I couldn't slow down.

Not again.

Not with Brooke.

Chapter 12

Brooke

"WHAT ABOUT THIS ONE?" LAKE ASKED, HOLDING UP A lovely gray and silver blouse. "It'll give you great cleavage." She beamed at me, and I held back a laugh.

"Are you trying to get me to show off my boobs to your cousin? When did we cross that friendship line?" I asked.

Lake laughed and tossed me the shirt before going to my closet.

I could've found something to wear on my own. I had been doing it daily for most of my life. But it was nice getting ready for our dates together. She was heading out soon to meet Zach, and Leif would be here soon to pick me up.

Luke rushed in. "I love it, Mommy! May is letting me have cookies later after we color. Is it really okay?"

I leaned down and brushed his hair from his face. "You know it. Just make sure you try to save me one, okay?"

Luke hugged me tightly, nodded, then ran back out to the living room past a smiling May in the door. May waved at me and followed Luke.

While I had mom guilt for leaving, I knew Luke was excited to be able to eat cookies tonight. He didn't get cookies every week, so being able to go on a sugar high tonight was his reward for a good week at school and to ease my guilt for leaving him to go on a date.

I knew I needed to have a life, that dating was part of that life, and I wasn't a terrible mom for doing this. It wasn't like I went out every night or left Luke to fend for himself. But that mom guilt was trademarked for a reason.

Lake came to my side and bumped hips with me. "That is one cute kid. And by the way? Leif is not my cousin right now. He is the guy you're going on a date with. So what if I want to show off your boobs to him? They are great boobs."

I laughed and quickly changed shirts, agreeing that the silver and gray one looked nice. It was a wrapped shirt that curved in at the waist and flared out slightly at my hips. It did indeed show off my cleavage, but not so much that I would feel a draft. "Okay, you win. I like this shirt. I don't know why I don't wear it often."

"Probably because even though you just moved in, it was still stuck in the back of your closet."

"You're probably right. I try to look somewhat nice for work, but I shouldn't show off the girls there."

"You could under your lab coat." Lake grinned. "It might be fun."

I rolled my eyes as I went to finish my makeup, feeling like a giddy teen getting ready for a date rather than the single mother who worked hard and too late some nights.

"I think slacks and a button-up shirt are just fine for under my lab coat."

Lake shook her head. "Do people even call them slacks anymore?"

I flipped her off good-naturedly. "No. Maybe it's a California thing."

"You live in Colorado now, so you're going to have to get with the lingo."

"Whatever you say. Although I didn't realize Coloradans had an accent. I distinctly remember someone saying that Colorado had a lack of accent, and that's why you could always tell who is from here."

"Maybe in the past. But so many people moved here in the past couple of decades that it's not that way anymore. We say y'all just like everybody else." Lake winked as she said it and fluffed her hair in the mirror as she stood beside me. "I need to go out and meet Zach, so he's not waiting for me. I hate making him wait for me."

I looked over at her and smiled. "So, you two are doing well then?"

Lake smiled brightly, her eyes shining, that I could see the happiness there without her even having to answer. "We are. He's just so nice. And kind. And he always makes sure that I have everything I need, especially after a long day or after I've been traveling. It's just nice to have someone to lean on, you know?"

I shook my head as I picked up my purse and followed Lake out of my bedroom and towards the living room. "Not really. I've been alone for a while." I hadn't meant to say that, but it was easy to be honest with Lake.

"I would say you're not alone anymore, but I mean the fact that I'm in your life. I'm not talking about your date."

"I appreciate that. It's just a date." I let out a breath. "And I don't know a lot about dating. I'm still learning. And Luke doesn't know."

Lake nodded, an understanding look in her eyes. "You're a good mom. I don't know how I would ever be able to handle bringing up dating to my son or daughter. And I know that Leif isn't going to begrudge you for acting as if he's just your friend in front of your son. There are delicate steps to be taken, and you're traversing them well."

"I don't feel like I am."

"You are." Lake froze as she looked at her phone and winced. "And that's Zach. I'm late. I've got to go. He's waiting for me." She practically ran out of the house, and I raised my brows, wondering why she had to dash to meet him. Maybe she just wanted to be with him. I could understand that. They were still in the beginning stages of the relationship, getting to know one another, and she didn't want to spend any time without him.

It was nice. And though I would like to think I wouldn't run to go meet Leif, I figured that probably wasn't the case.

"Mommy?" Luke asked, and I turned, an odd note in his voice sending up my mom alert.

"What is it, baby?"

May rushed out, her eyes wide, as Luke bent over and vomited on my shoes.

I held back a curse, lifted Luke into my arms, and carried him into the bathroom, thankful that we made it to the toilet before he vomited again.

"I'm so sorry. He was fine, and then he wasn't. I don't think he has a fever. I just felt him." May got a washcloth and ran it under cold water before handing it to me.

Luke began to cry, and I brushed his hair back

from his sweaty face, whispering sweet words to him. I lay the washcloth over his forehead and rubbed his back as he vomited again. I sat down next to him, my vomit-covered shoes next to me on the ground.

"Thank you, May. Can you get me the thermometer?"

"On it." She rushed out of the bathroom as I held my baby close, and he curled into a ball on my lap.

I was now covered in sweat and things I didn't want to think about, my pretty shirt probably ruined.

But that was fine. My baby was sick, and my mom guilt hit full force.

May came back with a thermometer, and as we took his temperature, noticed it was ninety-nine, and I sighed.

"Okay, buddy, let's keep you cleaned up and tucked into bed."

"You want me to call the pediatrician?" May asked, her eyes filled with worry but her tone steady.

I shook my head. "I can handle this. Why don't you head on home? I've got this."

"No, it's okay. I can help."

"You have a long day tomorrow, and we might have an even longer one depending on how tonight goes. You get some sleep so hopefully you don't end up sick, too." I cringed as I said it, and she nodded tightly.

"If you're sure. Let me know if you need anything. I'm just a phone call away."

I looked up at her, rubbing Luke's back. "I couldn't do this without you. Thank you, May."

"I'll clean up the mess before I go and try to do something with your shoes."

She didn't let me protest, and it wasn't like I could stop her, not with Luke in my arms, crying softly that his tummy hurt. I didn't think it would be too bad, at least I hoped not. There had been a stomach bug going through kindergarten for the last week, and I had hoped it had skipped Luke. Apparently, he was just a late bloomer.

By the time I cleaned up Luke and tucked him into bed, May had tidied up and headed home reluctantly.

I pulled off my shirt, treated it with a stain guard, and walked into my bedroom, wearing only a bra and panties. I quickly shoved on a shirt and shorts and cursed aloud as the doorbell rang.

Crap. I completely forgot I had a date.

How could I have forgotten Leif?

I walked past Luke's room, grateful he was still sleeping and looking better already, and then I ran to the front door, belatedly remembering I looked like hell.

My hair was piled on the top of my head, my makeup was probably running through sweat and tears, and I looked like I had been through the wringer.

I opened the door and cringed. Because there Leif was, looking sexy as hell in gray pants, a stone-gray button-up shirt, and those bright blue eyes of his looking far too damn good.

"Hey there. Did I get the night wrong?" he asked as he reached forward and tucked a piece of hair behind my ear.

I wanted to cry, but I knew I didn't have the right to do so. My baby was sick, and I did not have the time to break down.

"I'm sorry. Luke came down with a stomach bug, and I'm just now finished cleaning up and tucking him in. I completely forgot to text you and cancel. I'm so sorry. That must make me look like an idiot."

Leif's eyes widened and he walked in, closing the door behind him. He cupped my face and pressed his forehead to mine. "Are you okay? How is Luke? You need to take him to the doctor?"

I nearly burst into tears with how caring he was, the fact that he was so worried about Luke. Was my bar set so low for men that him just asking about my son nearly broke me?

"I'm okay. I'm just sorry to have made you come here for nothing. Luke is sleeping now, but I'm going to go in and check on him."

Leif pulled back and brushed my hair from my face again. "Why don't you go sit with him. I'll make you something to eat."

My eyes widened. "You don't want to leave? This isn't what you were expecting."

"I was expecting to spend time with you. And I can still do that, just with taking care of Luke. He's your son. Your number one priority. And he's sick. It's got to be scary and nerve-wracking. So, you take care of your kid because I want to make sure he's okay, too. I like that kid. So, let me make you dinner with whatever you have, and as long as you're okay with that, we can sit and eat together while keeping an eye on Luke."

My heart did that lurching thing, and I swallowed hard. "This wasn't what you were expecting tonight, Leif. Maybe this is all too much between work and life and family. You shouldn't be getting a single mom. You should be out there living your life, and actually be with somebody that can focus on you and only you."

Leif laughed and it made me wonder why the hell he was laughing. "I don't live in a dream world where nobody has any baggage or connections or life beyond my every whim and desire. You're a mom. I knew going into this that Luke is, and will always be, your number one priority. Sure, we could have gone out to eat tonight, and maybe I could've convinced you to kiss me, and maybe a little bit more," he said with a wink, and I laughed despite myself. "But that's not what's going to happen now. Instead, I will cook you something relatively edible, eat it maybe with some candlelight, and keep a look out all night. You do not have to worry about me, Brooke. I'm here. I'm not going anywhere."

With that, he kissed me hard on the mouth and then walked into the kitchen as if he had been doing it his whole life. I stood there, swallowed hard, and wondered why I was crying.

Because tears wet my cheeks at the thought of Leif just being nice to me and understanding, of liking my son and wanting to make sure that I was there for him. I wanted to be there for him as well.

I did not deserve Leif Montgomery. But I wanted to.

———

WE ENDED UP EATING BOX MACARONI AND CHEESE with my open bottle of rosé wine, sitting on the floor in my living room and talking quietly. I kept my video surveillance of Luke on my phone.

"His fever is already down, and he is sleeping hard. I think it was just a nasty little bug that should be over by the morning, but it scared me." I'd cleaned myself up a bit more, washing my face clear of makeup and putting my hair in a better messy bun. I still wore my bra and panties underneath a T-shirt and shorts, so it wasn't precisely date attire, but I felt comfortable.

I hadn't even slept with Leif yet, not since Paris, and yet here I was, having dinner with tea light candles lighting up the living room, and box macaroni and cheese as our gourmet meal.

It felt like home.

That should scare me, but it just felt right. I could think about everything that was wrong with it later.

"It scared me, too. I'm glad he's going to be okay."

I played with the rim of my wine glass, swallowing hard. "I know this isn't what you planned for tonight."

"I planned on spending time with you, Brooke. That's exactly what we're doing."

His eyes went dark, ever so slightly, and I bit my lip, noticing the way that his gaze went straight to the movement.

"You surprise me every day, Montgomery."

He smiled then, his gaze brightening. "I could say the same about you, Dr. Adler." He rose. "Oh, I'm going to have to call you Dr. Adler when I'm deep inside you."

I pressed my thighs together, holding back a groan. There was just something about this man. "Oh really, you're already imagining it?"

He leaned forward, brushed his lips to mine. "I imagine it every day. I'm hard enough most days that I have to begin my morning and end my night coming in my own damn hand thinking about you. And that might make me a growly asshole for daring to tell you that to your face, but I'm just going to have to lay it all out there. I want you to come on my cock. I want you to ride my face. I want to remember exactly what you look like when you orgasm. Even if it takes another year to get there, I want to know it all."

I swallowed, memories hitting me hard of what we had done in the past and what he put into such descriptive words.

I honestly could not think of a reason to wait.

So I wouldn't.

"It will not take another year," I said as I watched his throat work and swallow hard. "In fact, if you promise to keep quiet, it won't take another minute."

Then I leaned forward and kissed him harder. He groaned, the tension in the room shifting into something hot, primal.

He slid his hand over my hair, taking it out of its bun. It tumbled down my shoulders. He wrapped it around his fist, tugging ever so slightly.

I parted my lips, letting his tongue slide along mine as he deepened the kiss. I slid my hands up his back, over his shirt, and gently scratched my nails down the linen covering his muscled arm.

"Are you sure?" he asked, his voice a guttural moan.

"As sure as I'm ever going to be," I whispered. Probably not the best answer, but the truthful one. When he pulled back and looked at my face, I saw him searching, needing to know. But this was the moment. The only moment.

So I pulled away, noting the curiosity in his gaze

and how I stood up and pulled him with me. "Be quiet, very quiet," I whispered, winking.

He grinned and followed me to the bedroom. The bedroom was still slightly messy from getting ready with Lake, but it wasn't as bad as it could've been. But in the end, it didn't even look like he studied my room. Instead, he cupped my face again and deepened the kiss. The door was closed behind us, my phone in my hand. He took the phone from me, put it on the bedside table, and gently lifted me by my hips. My eyes widened at the show of his strength, subtle as it was, before he set me on the bed and kissed me harder. This time there was a sense of urgency as if we both knew if we weren't quick enough, if we didn't touch each other in the need that we held, this moment would shatter.

So I pulled at his buttons, undoing his shirt clumsily. We laughed as we both pulled away and he helped me undo the rest of his shirt. He tossed it to the floor, leaving him naked above the waist with nothing but ink.

I slid my hands down his chest, unable to hold myself back anymore. His skin seared mine, all hot and hard over sleek muscle. I sucked in a breath as I looked up at him, his eyes nearly glowing with need.

"Touch me, Brooke. I love when you touch me." He leaned forward, brushed his finger along my jaw. "I need you to touch me."

"Only if you touch me," I whispered, far more brazen than I thought possible. I knew we needed to be quiet, oh so quiet, so when he leaned down and gently lifted my shirt up over my head, I had to press my lips together so I wouldn't moan aloud.

I couldn't think then as he leaned down and kissed me, his hands on my breasts over the lace of my bra, then down my sides and over my hips. I pushed back onto the bed, needing him as I pulled him on top of me. He obliged, hovering over me and between my legs, and he kissed me in long, sure motions as if he had all the time in the world and he wasn't burning up from the inside out like I was.

Waiting.

Needing.

Aching.

Then his hand was between my legs over the thin cotton of my shorts, and I felt as if I were on fire. I arched into him, silently demanding more as he rubbed me over my shorts. When he finally, *finally*, slid his hands under the band to cup me, I nearly shot off the bed. It was only the fact his mouth was on mine that kept my moan contained.

This was so familiar, as if the two of us hadn't spent a decade apart, and yet it was all new and needy and everything I wanted and craved.

"That's it, Brooke. Ride my hand. Let me look at those pretty eyes as you drench my palm."

At the deep growl of his words, I nearly came. "Leif."

"It's just you and me." Then he slid his thick fingers deep inside me and curled them, my wetness making me so slick that he eased in without any resistance. "Fuck. You're so fucking wet, Brooke. Did I do that to you? Did I make this pretty pussy all wet and eager for me?" He began to work his fingers deep inside me, stretching me carefully. The sounds of my slickness over his hand nearly made me blush, but then he flicked my clit with his thumb, and it was hard for me to think.

I came on his hand as he worked me, his gaze greedy and pleased as I whispered his name, trying to keep quiet.

"That's it, Brooke. You're so pretty when you come. I need you to do it again. Can you do that for me, baby? Can you come on my hand?"

I shook my head, and he quirked a brow.

"Oh?"

"I want to come on your face," I said boldly, my cheeks so bright red they flamed.

He looked at me, his eyes wide, then he laughed before crushing his mouth to mine. I hadn't meant to say the words, but I couldn't help but imagine his face between my legs, the roughness of his beard along the inner silk of my thighs. Everything ached, and my pussy pulsated, needing more, needing him.

He moved us both, sliding off my shorts fully, then my bra.

He did the same to his pants and I swallowed hard, finally seeing all of him for the first time in years.

"When did you get your dick pierced?" I squeaked, my eyes going wide.

He looked down at himself, his cock hard, long, and thick with a barbell at the tip. "I've had it for a few years. I forgot that you haven't seen me since Paris." He met my gaze and stroked himself, once, twice.

I nearly came right then.

"Did it hurt?"

"A little, but not too badly. It'll feel good, Brooke. And I have condoms with me that are made for the piercing, so you don't have to worry about it breaking over it. I had it with me just in case. I promise I didn't think tonight would end like this."

I bit my lip, not realizing I was cupping my breasts and staring at his dick until he stroked himself again.

"You ready, Brooke?"

I nodded, licking my lips. "Always."

Then he was over me again, and his mouth was between my legs. I arched off the bed, slamming my hand over my mouth as he licked my pussy, sliding his tongue between my folds as he dove deeper. He spread me, blowing cool air over my heated flesh before he was licking and sucking and nearly sending me over the edge. When he shook his head slightly, humming along my clit and holding my thighs apart, feasting as if a man starved, I slid my free hand over his head, keeping him in place as I came, holding back another moan in case I shook the house with my screams.

Leif was over me then, as if I'd blacked out at that moment, his mouth on mine. I could taste myself on his lips, and I nearly came again. Instead, I wrapped my legs around him, needing him.

He pulled back, shaking his head before he moved to grab the condom I hadn't realized he'd placed near us.

I let out short, choppy breaths as he slid the condom over his length, his gaze never leaving mine.

"Brooke. You're gorgeous when you come. You're all pink and rosy. I can't wait to fuck you hard into this mattress. Do you think you can be quiet, baby? For me? Can you be quiet when I pound hard into you and make you come around my dick?"

I spread my thighs, slowly playing with my folds. "I think if you don't move and make good on those promises, I'm going to make myself come and never touch your cock. As it is, you've been selfish and haven't let me…play."

Again, I didn't know this Brooke. She sounded like the girl she had been in Paris, not the single mom she was now.

But that was what Leif did to me, and I didn't care. Not now, and maybe not ever.

And then Leif was between my legs and slowly, oh so slowly, sliding inside me. He was big, bigger than I remembered as he kissed me and slid deep inside me. He stretched me, the burn and ache, perfection. And when he was seated, I could feel the piercing within me, and the sensation was new, dangerous, and everything I hadn't known I'd wanted. Everything I hadn't known I'd needed.

And when he moved, taking his time, and not going hard and fast as he'd said, I knew this was rightness.

We crested over the abyss together, his hands and mouth on me as he shifted, so I was over him, riding him and rocking my hips. When he came, he held me close, kissing me as if there were no tomorrow, no yesterday, and only this moment forever.

I hadn't realized I was crying until he kissed my tears away and rubbed my back.

I looked at him then, and there were no words.

There didn't need to be.

I was falling for Leif Montgomery.

Again.

And I wasn't sure I could stop myself even if I wanted to try.

Chapter 13

Brooke

SOMEHOW, IN THE MONTH SINCE LEIF AND I HAD TAKEN that next step in our relationship, I only got to see him in stolen moments. We were both busy between our jobs and families.

I wished there were more moments where we could just be calm together. And I knew that would be easier once I introduced Luke to Leif as my boyfriend rather than just a friend. That would have to be soon because I wanted to spend as much time as possible with my son and Leif.

I hadn't realized that I would want to be in a relationship as quickly as it had come about, but there was no turning back. Because we were trying to find our happy middle, whatever that was.

However, none of that was important at the moment because I needed to finish getting ready for work and had to head to class. I had to teach, and then I had a meeting with a few advisors, and then there was research. Some professors didn't enjoy the teaching aspect and only wanted to do research. While for others, it was the opposite. I enjoyed both, which surprised me, but it added work to my already over-loaded plate. I felt like I was doing a million things at once. But I juggled it.

It was like what Nora Roberts, one of my favorite romance authors, had once said. You can juggle as many balls as you want. Just remember which balls are glass and which are plastic. The glass ones will shatter, so you don't want to drop them. So that would be Luke and maybe Leif—which was a terrifying thought.

The plastic ones, though, could bounce. And I wasn't saying that was my career, but if I let my postdoc and team work on items like they were supposed to rather than micromanaging them, that was okay.

"Mommy, you look pretty."

I looked to see Luke standing in the doorway, his smile bright, his dark hair falling over his eyes.

"Why, thank you. We need to get you a haircut."

"I was just putting that on the list," May put in, a

bright smile on her face. "Only because it's getting in front of his eyes. I kind of like it long in the back."

"Yes, because mullets are so in," I said with a laugh.

"I don't know. I'm starting to see kids with mullets. They could be in fashion. On trend, if you will."

I shuddered. "Okay. Whatever makes everybody happy. We do need to cut those bangs, buddy," I said as I knelt and hugged Luke tightly.

"It's okay. I like spiky hair."

"We could do spiky hair."

"What about the mohawk?"

I shook my head, laughing along with May. "I don't think so, Luke. Maybe a faux-hawk. Are those in?" I asked May.

"I have no idea. I think I will do some research today when he's in school before I pick him up."

May and Luke had an early day today thanks to teacher meetings. I liked being able to drop him off at school, and sometimes pick him up depending on my schedule, today was not going to be one of those days, but it was okay. We were making it work, and I wouldn't be able to do it without May. If it weren't for the fact that I had gotten a settlement from Luke's father and life insurance from my parents, I wouldn't be able to afford it, even with my good job. So I had to count what blessings I had.

I kissed the top of his head again and said goodbye as May and Luke went off to finish breakfast.

My car was parked in the driveway because we had an art project drying in the garage, so I walked out the front door and paused at the sight of Leif standing in my neighbor's yard, frowning at something.

"I didn't know you were going to be here."

I tried not to sound flushed or giggly. But it was hard to do with him around. Whenever I was near him, I wanted to touch, kiss, or just hear him laugh. I knew I was falling, and I had to be smarter about that. If nobody was around, nobody would know.

Except for the fact that we were in my front yard, and everyone would know.

Leif looked up at me, surprise etched on his features. "Hey, I would've stopped by, but I thought you would already be on your way to work. I know it's Luke's half-day, so I didn't want to confuse him by showing up early."

I smiled at that, loving the fact that he remembered. My heart did that wanting thing, and I pushed it away. I had to slow down. It would be smart to slow down.

"I'm heading to work now. I don't have class until later this morning."

I stood next to him on the driveway and tilted my head up as he kissed me, gripping my chin, just a soft good-morning kiss.

It felt…*everything*. That was probably the wrong thing to think, but I wasn't going to think about anything else right then.

"Anyway, I'm here because Lake needed me to water her plants, and I'm on my way to work. She should be back in town soon, but she asked me to come over."

"I could handle that. She shouldn't have to ask you."

"I know, but I think she just wanted me to come over just in case I could see you. My cousin is sly like that."

I laughed; I couldn't help it. "That sounds like Lake. If you need to water the plants, why are you outside?"

"Because I don't know if she wanted me to water these new roses, even though the sprinklers are on a timer. They look fine, but my aunts and uncles are way better at the whole gardening thing than I am."

"I'm honestly not great at it, but the flowers look fine. Nothing looks wilted, so maybe just the indoor plants?"

"Good to know that neither one of us has the green thumb in this relationship. We will have to hire someone in the future for our lawn needs. Because I don't think it will be either one of us."

He continued to talk about something else, and I listened with only half an ear. Because he had just casually mentioned the future, as if it was certain we would be living together, dealing with gardening together. Or maybe he was thinking of two separate homes like we were doing now.

I didn't need to think too deep about his words. Not when I was trying to rein myself in as I was.

"I need to go to work."

"No worries. Have fun." He kissed me softly and I held back a moan.

"I'm going to try. I have to deal with Grouchy Dude again today, not in the mood."

He narrowed his eyes. "Grouchy Dude? Why haven't you mentioned him before?"

I winced. I had been good about not bringing home that part of work before, mostly because I didn't want to deal with Landon outside of the office, but there was no taking it back.

"It's just a normal man and science thing. He gets annoying because he wanted my job."

"Idiot man," Leif said with a laugh, and I grinned. "How can you not like a woman in science? At least my woman in science. Makes me all tingly." He leaned forward and kissed me again, and I laughed against his lips.

"Thank you for that." I rolled my eyes, and I knew he was thinking about Landon. Leif wasn't going to handle it for me, he trusted me enough to know my own worth and process, but I also knew he was all growly because he wanted to handle things for me.

We were trying to figure out a balance, but I also knew it wasn't his problem.

We said our goodbyes, and I tried not to watch him as I drove away, knowing that we hadn't been careful then. Anyone could've seen us kiss, which was fine because it wasn't like I was hiding my relationship, except that my son could've looked outside at any moment and seen me kiss Leif. And that was something that I needed to deal with. Because I didn't want to lie to Luke. And I didn't want to hide Leif. Leif was worth more than that. It just meant things were going to get complicated. I had never brought a man home before. And though I had brought Leif home multiple times, it was never in the context of Luke knowing exactly what was going on.

I knew there were countless blogs and books about how to go about this, but those situations weren't my situation. I was going to have to figure out what to do. That was, of course, after my long day.

I enjoyed the drive, even in traffic, because though the mountains were behind me, Denver was still such a gorgeous city. Soon the light rail would be out here, and I would be able to take mass transit rather than driving. I was looking forward to that, although I did love the drive itself.

I pulled into my spot and walked into the physics

department, nodding at a few people, and saw Patrice walking down the hall.

"Hey there," the older woman said, grinning at me. "I saw your latest proposal. It looks great."

My heart kicked up a beat. "Really? Okay, good. I swear I feel like a first-year sometimes with those."

Patrice laughed. "Same here. But you're not alone. And it looks great. I actually have a proposal for you that I want you to look at because I think we can work together on this latest thing." She looked at her phone. "I have to head to class, and I know you have one at ten a.m. But I do want to talk to you."

Everything just clicked. I had a work friend. She wanted to work together. It didn't feel like we were in competition. Well, that was a fantastic way to start the day.

"That sounds wonderful. And yes, we should meet up and talk. I would love to work together. I'm excited."

"I'm excited too. I was thrilled when they hired you on. I loved your work out at Caltech and even referenced it in my own papers."

I laughed, pleased. "I feel all proud right now. Seriously."

Patrice grinned, then headed off to class while I made my way to my office.

Things just felt right. I was making headway with my research. I had built my team, and my students were doing well. Yes, classes were difficult just with the grant scope, but I was getting the hang of it. And yes, I could probably sleep more if I didn't have so many papers to grade along with my TA, but it was fine. I was making do.

And maybe the next night, I would invite Leif over and we would have dinner with Luke. The three of us. When I didn't just have my friend over for dinner.

As if he were thinking about me, Leif texted, and I picked up my phone as I closed my office door behind me.

Leif: *Just thinking of you.*

Well then, that wasn't kismet or anything.

Me: *Hi.*

That was great—a great way to start off a texting conversation.

Leif: *Do you want to go to the farmers' market this weekend? Luke will love it.*

I bit my lip, now wondering if it was too quick. Yes, I'd just thought about bringing him over to dinner, but going out as a family seemed like too far. Or maybe I was thinking too deeply. It was just a farmers' market. It wasn't like I was asking him to move in. I needed to stop being indecisive and let things go with the flow. Damn it.

I swallowed hard, my palms going clammy.

Me: *That sounds great. I have a busy weekend coming up. Errands and haircuts.*

Leif: *I can help with errands. I work in the evenings both nights since I'm covering for Nick. But I can help.*

Me: *You don't have to help with errands. You have your own life.*

Leif: *I want to be part of yours. Luke knows I'm your friend. That's not going to change, Brooke. I'm not going to scare him.*

I swallowed hard, knowing that he was right. And our thoughts were going in the right direction. Just because he thought as I did, didn't mean I had to be scared.

Me: *Okay. Let's work on timing. And if you're not busy tonight, you should come to dinner.*

I practically threw my phone on the desk as I said that, knowing that that was taking a leap.

Leif: *See you tonight. I'll bring dessert if Luke is allowed to have sugar.*

Me: *Okay. You can just bring yourself, but I like dessert, too.*

Leif: *I have to go to work now, and I can't have a hard-on. So I'm not going to think about exactly how you can be a dessert for me.*

I rolled my eyes and set my phone down, shaking my head. He was just too much, yet he was still the same person he had been in Paris. The person that made me smile and always put others first. He was kind and talented and a little growly. But I liked that about him.

But I couldn't think about him when I needed to focus on work.

I picked up my things to head to class and just opened the door to find Landon standing there. For some reason my pulse jumped. It was just Landon. And yet there was something off about him when he narrowed his gaze at me.

"We need to talk."

He practically shoved me into my office and slammed the door behind him.

"Excuse me? What do you think you're doing?" My pulse sped up, and my mouth went dry. This was bad. Oh, so bad. My phone was still on my desk because I hadn't picked it up when I picked up my things, and he closed the damn door, locking us inside. I could call out for help, but everybody was either at their morning classes or not in yet. This was so stupid. I just had to calm him down. But he had pushed me. This could go only a few ways, and I didn't like any of them.

"I'm doing what I should've done to begin with. I should've had your job. But no, they had to go in and hire a woman because we don't have enough pussy here."

I held back a flinch at his tone, not wanting to show weakness.

"Landon, you're going to want to leave my office right now. This is highly inappropriate, you shouldn't be in here, and you should not talk to me that way." I was doing my best to sound professional, but inside I was screaming, wondering what the hell I was supposed to do.

"Bitch." He moved quickly, wrapping his hand around my throat and shoving me sideways into the door. My eyes widened and I sucked in a breath, only barely catching up to what he had just done. It took me a moment to figure out exactly what the hell was going on, and in that moment of being too slow, he got the upper hand.

"This is supposed to be my job. I was supposed to be on the tenure-track. Instead, they brought you in because they only had little Patrice. She's too old and fat for any of the professors to want. So they brought in this hot young thing to take my job. Well, screw that. You don't get to take what's mine. So I'm going to take what's yours." He slapped me then, shocking me. Red-hot pain slid up my face, my eyes watering.

"You stupid cunt." He slammed my shoulders against the door, his hand on my throat, the other gripping my shoulder so hard I knew I would bruise.

It took too long for my brain to catch up as he hit me again, but then I finally focused, taking the deepest breath I could with him still holding my throat. My hands were free, so I scratched at his face and lifted my knee, using that moment of distraction to knee him right in the balls. I pushed him down to the ground and tried to open the door. He scrambled up and gripped my hips, so I kicked back, elbowing him in the chest.

I opened the door and nearly fell out into the hallway, shouting for help.

"Help! Somebody help me! Landon has lost his mind. Help!"

I never yelled, I never asked for help, but my own pride would not stand in my way. I saw Patrice there, her eyes wide as she ran to me, phone in hand.

"Brooke? Oh my God."

Landon threw himself through door and looked ready to kick me before he saw other people coming out of their offices, all coming towards us.

I knew what this looked like, me practically on the ground, shaking, blood seeping from a cut to my lip. I knew my eyes were wild, my hair askew.

Landon looked like he'd stopped mid rage, his face nearly purple.

Then Patrice was on the phone, talking with 911. A few professors I couldn't name at the moment and Randall were holding Landon back, students ready to jump in.

Patrice was in front of me, holding my hand, asking me what happened, and I tried to catch up, try to let my brain unfreeze.

Everything went dark for a minute, and I swayed, and then Jennifer and Hannah were there, both holding me tight, keeping me steady. I tried to lift my chin and did my best to look as if I hadn't just been attacked in my own office. As if I wasn't bleeding or scared.

Because I would not be weak.

I could not be weak.

And then the tears came, and I let the women of the physics department hold me, and I tried to tell myself everything would be okay.

Even though I knew nothing would ever be okay again.

Chapter 14

Leif

ANGER ROLLED OFF ME IN WAVES, AND I DID MY BEST TO rein it in. Yelling at anybody in my path wasn't going to help anything. But it was all I could do not to see red and find this damn Landon person and beat the shit out of him. Violence had already come into her life. I wasn't going to add to it.

I fisted my hands at my side and took in a deep breath.

"She's fine, son. She's okay."

We sat in the waiting room in the hospital, something that we had done countless times when I was a kid, through various things with my aunts and uncles and parents. You would think I would be used to this by now, since we basically had our own Montgomery wing, and yet nothing felt right.

"I should be back there," I whispered.

My dad squeezed my shoulder and I let out a breath. "You will be. You know how it is, HIPAA restrictions and all that. As soon as you are able, I know you will be back there."

I looked at my dad, his big beard always comforted me. My dad had been through hell and back, a lot of it having to do with me. But he'd always been there for me—just like he had always been there for my siblings and my mom.

Sierra, not my birth mom. I tried not to think about my birth mom, but it was hard not to these days when my so-called stepdad/birth-mom's-boyfriend was back in the picture. Not that I was going to tell my dad about that. No, adding that on top of everything else wouldn't help anyone.

"I want to be there now. I want to know what's going on."

"You will know soon." My dad turned and I followed his gaze. "Good, here's your mom and Luke."

I stood up, practically scrambling to Luke.

May had met us at the hospital, Luke in tow, when we had heard about the incident at the university. I wanted to rush behind the nurse's counter and find Brooke, but I wasn't family and wasn't on her emergency contact list. Apparently, nobody was. That was going to have to change soon.

But May had left shortly after dropping off Luke, the right side of her face swollen from a badly needed root canal that popped up out of nowhere. Nick, of all people, had driven her to the dentist under protest. She hadn't wanted to go, had wanted to stay there with Luke to wait to hear more about Brooke, but we had all pushed her into leaving.

That meant Luke was with us in the waiting room, and I was thankful that my parents had come. Any one of my siblings, cousins, or numerous other family members would be here. But I hadn't wanted to overwhelm Brooke, considering she hadn't even officially met my family.

We had been dating for a few weeks now, and it seemed odd that I hadn't had her and Luke over for family dinner. Then again, Luke didn't even know we were dating. He just thought I was Brooke's friend.

Things were going to change after this. As soon as I made sure she was okay, she would have to realize how important she was to me.

I hadn't even realized the words rang true until they were practically spewing out of me. I only held it in because Luke was in front of me now, and I went to my knees, holding my arms out. Luke ran to me and nearly strangled me as he hugged me tightly.

"Is Mommy okay?"

I stood up, set Luke on my hip, and pushed his hair back from his face.

"She's going to be just fine." I hoped I was not lying. But if it was bad, she would've told me. She would've sent somebody out to tell me.

I hated not knowing. I hated not being her emergency contact. Because she was all alone back there, and here I was, holding Luke, and I didn't know what to say. I wasn't good at this. I wasn't a dad.

That thought made my mouth go dry.

I would do anything for her and Luke. I just had to figure out what all that meant. The fact that this was coming at me all at once nearly took the words from me, and it was hard for me to speak. Because I hadn't been prepared for this. I hadn't been prepared for her or Luke. I wasn't sure what the hell I was supposed to be doing.

"Luke enjoyed our little walk, and now he promised to go play with the puzzles in the back with me."

I looked up at my mom, and she smiled at me. There was such kindness in her gaze, even with worry. It reminded me of the first time she had been in the hospital when she had been hurt when I was a kid. But she was okay now, strong.

Brooke was just as strong. I had to remember that.

"I like puzzles," Luke said shyly as he looked over at Sierra. She smiled at him, and I knew that Luke was a goner. My mom had that way with kids. After all, I had fallen for her just like my dad had. I wanted her in my life, even before I knew that my dad wanted her, too. I was forever grateful that Sierra was my mom. That she had stood up and said her vows to my dad, holding my hand and making me promises as well.

That had been so long ago, yet I could still remember that day, the tears running down her face as she had promised to be the best mom she could be for me. And then she had cried again when the adoption papers had come through, and she was my mom in truth.

Luke looked over at her with that same knowledge, that same love.

"Let's go play puzzles while Leif and Austin go see what we can do about seeing your mom."

Luke buried his face into my neck, sighing. "I want my mommy to be okay."

My heart clutched, and I rubbed my hand on his back. "I want her to be okay, too." I pressed my lips together, knowing that probably was the best thing to say. "And she will be okay. We will figure out when we can see her, and then we will take her home. Then you and I get to have the fun job of ensuring that she's all tucked in and comfortable. What do you say?"

"And then we can all sleep in Mommy's bed and make sure she is safe?"

I did my best not to look at my parents as they met each other's gazes, holding back a laugh.

"We can make that happen." I kissed the top of Luke's head, then set him down as he went off to the children's area with my mom.

My dad gestured towards the nurse's station, but before I could go and harass them, albeit nicely, a woman in scrubs walked out and looked over at me.

"Leif Montgomery?"

My heart did double-time, and I swallowed hard. "That's me. Is it Brooke? Can I see her?"

She held up a hand, looking very serious. The floor fell out from beneath my feet, and I swayed. My dad squeezed my shoulder tight. He grounded me as always, and I swallowed hard.

"Just tell me."

The woman smiled, looking slightly tired. "She'll see you now, and she can tell you how she's doing."

I didn't know what to make of that, but maybe it was in the rules that because I wasn't Brooke's emergency contact, I wasn't allowed to know anything about how she was doing. I wasn't sure how I felt about that, but it didn't matter in the end. All that mattered was that Brooke would be fine, Luke and I would definitely talk her into resting, and make sure that she was safe and wrapped in bubble wrap.

And that I could find this Landon and beat the crap out of him.

My dad gave me a tight nod, squeezed my shoulder again, and then let go to walk over to where my mom and Luke were playing. I was glad for it. They would keep Luke occupied while I talked with Brooke.

I hated the fact that she was alone. But she wouldn't be for long. Damn it.

The doctor gestured towards a curtained-off room, and I nodded in thanks as I saw Brooke lying there, my body nearly failing me.

She looked so small, so fragile. Brooke never looked small. She always looked as if she could take on the world and did so every day. She was brilliant, a freaking doctor. She was an actual nuclear physicist who could take over the world. But she looked so fragile I was afraid that a stiff breeze could break her.

A bruise marred the side of her jaw, and at the narrowing of her gaze, I had a feeling she knew exactly where my thoughts were. She wouldn't want me to think she was fragile.

But I was so pissed off I couldn't even breathe. I wanted to shout and scream and make sure that she was okay. But that wasn't helpful.

Vengeance, my anger, it didn't matter what I was feeling.

"Brooke? Are you okay?" I blurted, my voice coming out with a growl. The nurse walking by gave me a look. I sucked in a breath and exhaled through my nose, telling myself to calm down.

"May said you had Luke." She held up her phone. "I'm sorry. I'm so sorry. You shouldn't have to take care of him. Just…you know, thank you."

I moved to her and reached out to touch her hand. She didn't flinch, didn't move away, but I saw the bruising on her throat, the cut on her forehead, on her lip. And I wanted to scream. But that wouldn't help.

I closed my eyes, counted to five, and opened them as I leaned forward. Her hair was pushed back from her face. She just looked so frail, and I hated that. I wasn't going to let myself think that. Not when she needed me to be strong. And yet it was all I could do not to growl.

"Luke is with my parents in the waiting room. He's fine. Worried about you, and he wants to see you."

Her eyes widened, her mouth parting. "He's with your parents? He's just alone with your parents."

My brows raised. "Lake is out of town, May is having oral surgery, and my parents have raised four kids. I trust them with my life."

"I don't know them." She closed her eyes and cursed. "I'm sorry. I've met your mother, she was lovely. Even though I didn't know she was your mother at the time, and it was only for a few minutes. I just can't believe they're putting everything aside to watch my son. I need to get out of here, need to go and see him."

"You will. As soon as you tell me what's going on."

"Don't tell me what to do, Leif. You're not my husband."

My eyes widened and that rage came right back. "Oh, so we're going to do this right now?"

"Do what?" she snapped.

"I might not be your husband, but we're together. You're mine just like I'm yours. And beyond all that, we are friends, Brooke. You know that."

"I am doing just fine on my own. I always have."

I sighed and pushed back the rage threatening to overtake me. "Yeah, you did just fine on your own. And you always will. But you do not *have to*. What would happen to Luke right now if my parents weren't out there? Where would you want him to go?"

"Stop it."

"Stop what?" I asked, exasperated. "Stop caring about you? That's not going to happen, Brooke. It can't."

"That has nothing to do with the situation. I got hurt. I'm fine. And thank you. Thank you for taking care of Luke. They will discharge me soon, and I can handle this."

I was quickly losing control of this conversation, and I needed to get us back on track before either one of us said something we regretted.

"What happened? Let's start there, and then we can go back to what you're yelling at me about. What I'm about to yell at you for."

"Don't go off on me."

"You're the one going off on me. I'm not being a jerk, Brooke. I am your friend. Your fucking boyfriend. Let me help." Tears filled her eyes, and I felt like an ass. "Brooke."

She shook her head. "I'm sorry. That guy at work got weird." She let out a rough laugh, and I understood because "weird" was the understatement of the year. "Apparently, he was drunk and he attacked me." She went into detail about everything that had happened, about her coworkers holding him and calling 911. How she'd already spoken to the authorities twice, all while thinking May could take care of Luke. And then May had called me. Not Brooke.

That hurt, but I understood. I did. Brooke was so used to doing everything on her own, so it made sense that she wouldn't reach out.

But things were going to have to change.

I was falling for her, and I damn well knew she was falling for me, too. So we couldn't pull away from each other. She had to rely on me, to lean on me, because if she didn't, what was the damn point?

"I want to kill him." I whispered the words I hadn't even realized I was saying until they were already out.

"The authorities will handle him. I don't want to make it a big deal. As it is, I have to go to work, to that same office where everybody will know that somebody hurt me. I have to be *that woman* with them. I don't want to be *that woman* with you."

The way that she emphasized *that woman* told me it was a whole other thing that she needed to deal with. I didn't know if I was the right person to help. Maybe my mom would be able to help. Maybe Lake. I would bring it up later, but first, I needed to touch her.

I leaned forward and cupped her bruised cheek. "You scared me, Brooke. You scared me so damn much."

Her eyes watered, and thankfully she leaned into my touch. Leaned in and didn't back away. I had to count that as a good sign.

"I was scared, too. I don't want Luke to see me like this."

I nodded, looking down at her hospital gown. "When are we breaking out of here?" I asked.

Her lips twitched, and she winced since one of them was cut. I held back a curse. "They said it would be another hour. I don't know what to do, Leif. I always know what to do."

I sat down next to her and gripped her hand. "Okay. Why don't my parents take Luke home?" She opened her mouth to argue, and I held up my hand. "May can't help right now, and it's understandable. She feels bad about that, by the way, so make sure you know that she tried her hardest to help. Nick had to practically drag her out."

Brooke's eyes widened. "She was in that much pain?"

"She tried to hide it from you because she was scared. For you and for herself, I think. But she's okay. She's going to be okay. Lake is touching down at the airport any minute now, and we have that transportation handled, but how about this? My parents take Luke home, give him a fun evening, and then you can video call him later. That way, he doesn't feel as scared. Then later, after we get you settled at home, we can bring Luke back, after dinner, after he gets spoiled by my parents, and see what happens then."

"I guess you have it all handled." She paused and frowned. "I'm not good at letting other people handle me, Leif. I've never been good at that."

I let out a rough chuckle. "I know. But it's okay. Because you're going to let me do this. You let me take care of you. I already promised Luke that I would help talk you into letting us take care of you." I raised a brow. "He also asked if we could all sleep together in your big bed to make sure you're okay." She sputtered, and I grinned. "Smart kid there."

"I don't know what to do, Leif. I was so scared. But I'm okay now. I'm going to be okay. I don't have a concussion. I didn't even need to get stitches. I am just a little banged up. And it took a while to get through the emergency room because of a pile up on the highway and then dealing with the authorities."

"You're going to be okay," I repeated, primarily for myself. "Luke and I will take care of you because we're your guys. It's what we do."

"Leif… I don't know what to say."

I sat up, leaned forward, and brushed my lips against hers. "Don't say anything. Just be okay, Brooke. Let us be there for you."

I kissed the tears away from her cheek and then held her hand as we waited. I needed her to lean on me. I just needed her.

But even as I thought the words, the fear of what happened to her hit me. Something so inconspicuous, something I hadn't even realized was a threat to her, hurt her.

And my own secrets, my own past, were still waiting.

I knew that if I didn't deal with it soon, the danger that blurred between us both wouldn't end here.

I just didn't know where that end would be.

Chapter 15

Leif

I FINISHED RINGING UP MY FINAL CUSTOMER OF THE DAY and looked over at my dad leaning against the wall, arms folded over his chest as he stared at me.

I knew that he wasn't judging me or staring at me to ensure that I did everything right. That was just the way that my dad leaned. He was big like I was, so we tended to take up room. To look intimidating without even trying. And yet, even as his son, I wasn't sure how I was supposed to not feel intimidated.

"I just love it, Leif. I can't wait to be able to show it off to the world."

I looked at Kathleen and grinned. "Just don't get

No.

arrested for indecent exposure when showing it off," I teased.

Kathleen rolled her eyes. "I may have gotten a bouquet of flowers in between my breasts, but I can still show it off with the right top. I promise not to flash random strangers on the street. But I'll tell them I got it at Montgomery Ink Legacy if I do. I'll be your bill-board." She winked and then waved at us with her fingers before strolling out of the place, singing a song to herself.

I shook my head, laughing softly as my dad joined in.

"That is good for business, a nice walking billboard."

"How many women have flashed you, Austin Montgomery?" Mom asked as she came up from the back, my portfolio in her hands. She had been in the office, on the phone with one of her suppliers while looking over my work.

"I plead the fifth," Dad said as he wrapped his arm around his wife's shoulders. "I don't want to incrimi-nate myself."

"Pleading the fifth only works in the court of law, not my court." She went to her tiptoes and kissed his cheek. "I'm sure you did lovely work, even as you were touching other women's breasts."

"I don't think I need to be here for this conversa-tion." I shuddered as they looked at me before we all burst out laughing.

"What did I miss?" Sebastian asked as he walked in, phone in hand as he practically bounced.

"Just talking about boobs," Mom said dryly.

Sebastian blushed. "Aunt Sierra, really?

"You asked," she said with a laugh. Then she moved around the counter and hugged Sebastian tight. "Why are you all bouncy?"

Sebastian wrapped his arms around her, looking down. I hadn't realized that my cousin was now taller than my mom. I should have, it was jarring.

From the way that my mom looked up, she felt it too.

"I had a good day. I got an A on my exam, thought of a kickass tattoo for later, and have a date with Marley tonight."

"I just love that girl. I know your parents do, too." Mom moved away and went back to my portfolio, keeping her attention on the group of us.

"I love her, too. One day soon, I'm going to marry her." Sebastian practically beamed, and I shook my head.

"Soon? As in how soon?"

My dad let out a sigh. "Give my brother some time to get used to the fact that his kids are grown before you go out and get married." And then Dad looked at me. "Of course, you have been grown for a while now. When are you going to ask Brooke?"

I choked on air and looked over at my dad. "What?"

"I love how his voice gets all high-pitched like that," Sebastian said. "And Marley and I want to wait until after college to get married. We can pay for the wedding ourselves and not beg my parents for money."

I noticed he hadn't mentioned Marley's parents. Marley's parents didn't like to spend money, didn't like parties, and didn't like Sebastian. Mainly because their baby girl was precious to them, and nobody would be good enough for her.

But that wasn't my problem. At least not until they hurt my cousin. Then I would make it my problem.

"That sounds like a plan," I said, being honest. "And as for Brooke and me, we're doing good. Taking it slow, but I like her. And Luke."

"I just hope that we get to meet her in a circumstance of our own choosing." Mom gave me a look, and I winced.

It had been a few weeks since the attack, physically Brooke had healed, and found her way. I knew she still needed to talk about it with someone else, to recover fully, but she was doing better.

The three of us were.

"I told you we're taking it slow." Even though I didn't believe that we were taking it too slow. Because we saw each other nearly every day, and I slept over at her house more often than not. She had yet to sleep at my house, and I understood. We hadn't wanted to leave Luke overnight, and while I had a guest room, I didn't have a room for Luke. I didn't think we were ready for that, and honestly, the complications made it too difficult. So I was fine sleeping at her place.

As long as she let me, I would sleep there as much as possible.

But marriage? I needed to make sure we were both ready.

"Anyway, so I don't stress you out about Brooke anymore, I was looking over your latest drawings for the art show. I love them. Have you shown your uncles?" Mom asked, speaking of my uncles who worked in art outside of the tattoo world.

"Uncle Alex and Uncle Jake both looked at them. I know that the gallery was interested in one. I'm fine with it as long as it hits the bank." I shrugged. "I love drawing, but I love what I'm doing here more. I'm doing okay."

"You're doing more than okay." Mom reached up and kissed my cheek, then cursed as she looked down at her ringing phone. "I need to take that."

"And I need to go look at my next project," Sebastian added as he gave us a two-finger salute and headed back to his station.

That left me alone with my dad while I waited for Nick to come in and start his shift and take care of any walk-ins.

"While the others are away, want to tell me why you're so stressed?" Dad asked.

I looked up at him, confused. "Why do you say that?"

He gave me a look that told me he once again could read me like no other. "Is it Brooke?"

Honestly, Brooke was the one thing in my life that was making sense. But I didn't need to tell my dad that. Maybe I did. Maybe I just needed to tell him what was going on. Only I saw the worry in my dad's gaze, saw the stress.

I knew that Gideon and Jamie took up most of their time these days outside of the business. They were fifteen now and ready to take over the world. Colin was twenty-one, finishing college soon. My parents stressed about a lot of things.

Roger calling me like he had that one time almost two months ago shouldn't be a problem. It shouldn't be something on my dad's shoulders, so I wouldn't mention it. I could handle it. I always had been able to handle those memories, and I would handle them in the future. But there was one thing I could mention. Because it was something I knew I needed to get over.

"Is it weird that I opened a tattoo shop just like you? Following in your footsteps even though I didn't mean to?"

Dad's eyes widened, looking honestly surprised. Hell, I was surprised I'd even said the words. "Is that what you think? That you have to live up to our expectations? Because that's not it. I thought you wanted to open up this place. To have your own business and not work with me or for me. Did I push you in a direction you didn't want? Fuck, Leif."

I shook my head and ran my hands through my hair. "I'm not saying it right."

"Then tell me. Did we do something to force you into this? I know your mom is just talking about your other art because she loves your talent. Same as I do. Drawing and clay and other media like you do never appealed to me as an artist, never did. But you have always been so talented with it all. You didn't have to follow in my footsteps. Not that I thought you would."

I shook my head. "I don't know. I'm the oldest cousin. I always felt like living up to what Montgomery Ink is, could be a little daunting." I let out a sigh. "I know it's stupid."

My dad shook his head and squeezed my shoulder. "Look at all you've accomplished on your own. *And* with family. I had my family. I might've tried to forget that when I was your age, but in the end, you and I are both blessed with this big damn family. You are your own man. You always have been. You've grown into someone that I will always admire and trust. Breathe, okay? This place has its own reputation outside of the place Maya and I made with our friends. One day we will retire, a long ways away, boy, which means we will have a place for every Montgomery who wants to join us. Or do whatever they want. You have always been who you wanted to be. I admire the man you've become, and the art you create, on canvas or on skin. You have the talent, the drive, and the trust. Don't worry about what we think but know that we think the world of you."

My throat tightened, and I tried not to react to every single word my father had just said.

"What the hell is wrong with me?" I said after a moment, laughing. "I know you guys are proud of me. You guys have never once pushed me in any direction I didn't feel comfortable with. And as for Brooke, by the way, you're not going to be able to force her into a Montgomery dinner."

"I might the next time we see her. Only because it's been long enough. But it's not like we found where she worked and asked her there," Dad said after a minute.

I laughed. "I need to invite her to a family dinner. She's just been busy, and well, we wanted time."

"I get you." Dad ran a hand over his beard. "You're at a crossroads. With your woman. Your new life. Of course, you will be filled with doubt. But you have your friends. Your family. Lean on us. It's okay to lean."

I smiled and reached out to hug my dad hard. There were many things to say about Austin Mont-gomery, but he always gave good hugs.

"I love you, kid. Just saying."

"Can I get a hug, too?" Sebastian asked, and I rolled my eyes and turned, pulling my cousin into the hug.

Sebastian laughed, then pushed away. "I meant from Uncle Austin. You're fine, but your hugs need work."

I push at his shoulder, laughing, as the three of us roughhoused playfully.

My mom came out of the back office and rolled her eyes. "Seriously, I leave the three of you alone for five minutes, and now you're fighting."

"You love me," my dad said, and Mom laughed as the bell above the door jingled, and the woman who took my breath away walked in.

I swallowed hard, trying to get my thoughts in order so I wouldn't drool. But that was really hard to do when Brooke was there, looking sunny and amazing, with her hand in Luke's.

"Oh, my," Brooke said, her eyes wide.

"Leif," Luke called out and ran towards me. Brooke reached for him but missed, so I went around the counter and scooped Luke up in my arms.

"Hey there, buddy. You're looking smooth in that sweater."

Luke beamed. "Mom picked it out."

"She did a good job." I looked over Luke's head at Brooke. "Hi."

"Hi." She clutched her hands in front of her, nervous. She looked behind me at my family, who was staring, grins on their faces.

I cleared my throat and knew it was time to stop hiding her in our bliss and confusion. "You know everybody here, but let me do introductions anyway," I said as I kissed the top of her head, holding her close.

"Okay, Luke, that is my mom, and dad, and my cousin Sebastian. Everybody, this is Luke and Brooke. You've mostly all already met, but now it's not in a stressful situation."

My chest filled with pride as Luke waved to everybody and then scrambled down so he could go and say hello to Sebastian. Sebastian picked the kid up, settled him on his hip, and proceeded to hear all about Luke's day.

Brooke just laughed and came forward. "Well, we see where we place in terms of hierarchy here," she said dryly.

"It's the Montgomery boys. You just can't help it." Mom came out from behind the counter along with Dad, and she hugged Brooke tightly.

"It's good to see you. I was trying to give you space because I didn't want to overwhelm you. We Montgomerys tend to do that." She winked, and Brooke laughed. "However, we're ready for the next phase, so here it goes."

"Now I'm worried," Brooke said, her eyes wide as she looked at me.

Mom waved her off. "Don't be. We're just inviting you to a Montgomery dinner."

Sebastian whistled between his teeth, and I narrowed my gaze at him as I looked over at Brooke. "It won't be all the Montgomerys. Not even close. Literally just my immediate family. No extra cousins, aunts, and uncles."

"Hey, that's not nice," Sebastian whined.

"That's what I was thinking," Sierra said dryly. "I was thrust into the lion's den of Austin's seven siblings. Since Leif only has three siblings, you are getting off easy here."

Austin Montgomery snorted. "I feel like I should apologize for that, but I can't. I like my family. And I promise my parents won't be there either, even though they want to meet you."

Brooke's eyes widened, and she laughed, looking at all of us. "I know that Nick told Leif that he needs to get me a family tree so I can get all the names right. I thought he was kidding."

"You'll be fine. I still mess up," Mom said with a laugh.

Brooke rolled her shoulders back. "Okay, dinner sounds good. I wanted to invite you guys over for dinner at my place anyway, just to say thank you."

The reasons why were left unsaid, and I knew it

was because Luke was there and probably because nobody wanted to mention the subject.

"We can do your place next. This is fun. I can't wait. You'll have to tell me any allergies you have." Then my mom went still. "And if you like cheese. These are things I need to know."

Brooke threw her head back and laughed. I just grinned as Luke clapped and Sebastian chuckled. "Oh, I know all about the Montgomerys and cheese. I hear that, along with tattoos, are your favorite vices."

"Guilty," Dad said, deadpan.

"I love cheese. As does Luke. Right, buddy?"

Luke smacked his lips together. "Cheese is the best."

"That's what I like to hear," my dad said as he held up a hand. Luke looked at it curiously before he high-fived it, and my dad grinned.

As Mom and Brooke talked a bit more, I went over to listen to Sebastian and my dad joke around with Luke. I stayed quiet, watching them, and swallowed hard.

This felt right, like a family. I didn't want anything to break it. I couldn't. That meant I needed to deal with one last thing before I could take that next step. Only I wasn't sure exactly how to do that.

My parents left before too long, Brooke and Luke leaving soon after, which left me alone with Sebastian while we waited for Nick to show up to work.

"I hear there's a Montgomery dinner in order," Nick put in as he set his stuff down at his station.

I glared over at Sebastian. "It's been like ten minutes."

Sebastian shrugged. "I only texted Lake. She texted the rest of the family group chats."

I pulled out my phone and cursed at the twenty-nine notifications. "My God."

"It's a big thing, bringing a girl and her kid over for dinner," Sebastian said sagely.

"My family is going to give me gray hair," I said with a laugh and then froze as someone else walked into the shop.

He looked different, and yet the same. Twenty years had passed, but I had looked up his picture once I was notified of his release so I would be able to recognize him. Gray hair, strong jaw, thick nose. He was big now because he had used the prison yard to stay in shape. He still looked mean and smarmy and like the man who had made my life hell when I was a kid.

And then he was taken away, and Mom died, and I ended up with Austin. In the end, it all worked out, but I never wanted to think about him.

Or fucking look at him.

"What are you doing here?" I asked as both Nick and Sebastian stood up. They both had clients, regulars who looked up and narrowed their eyes, noticing the tension. This was my place of business, and I didn't want this to be a big thing, but I wasn't sure what else to do.

"I just wanted to see where my kid worked."

"I'm not your kid. Mom never married you. You're just some guy she was with. Then you were in prison. You need to go now. This is my place of business, and I don't want you here."

Did I sound calm? Because I didn't feel calm.

"I just thought you owed me. Don't you think you owe me? You have all of this while I was sent to prison. Doesn't really seem fair."

"You were sent to prison for your own actions and decisions that had nothing to do with me."

"Yet you have such a good life, but where would you be without me?"

"You have nothing to do with who I am. You need to go."

"Maybe I should go see that girl, the one that just left here with the pretty hair and eyes. What about that little kid? Your mom was about that age when I met her. You were about that kid's age, too. Brings back memories."

I moved forward, my fist flying out without even thinking. But then Nick was there, holding me back.

"This is just what he wants," Nick whispered in my ear.

"Got yourself a boyfriend holding you back, too? Well, I knew things got weird in your family. I didn't realize that you were one of them."

I pushed forward, but Nick held firm. "Get your hate speech and dickishness out of here."

"That's just fine. If you're not going to help me, maybe she will. She looks rich. I'll see what she wants to do to help a poor man."

"Stay away from her."

"Maybe I will, maybe I won't. She reminds me of your mom. Be nice to see her."

Then Roger walked out, and I sucked in a breath, my gaze going fuzzy.

"You need to call the family," Nick whispered as their clients got up and came forward.

Brett, a big man and construction worker that worked with my family, narrowed his gaze. "You need to call your parents. Seriously, at least let them know. And the cops."

"Brett's right," Jared put in. He was a fireman, worked long hours, and was one of Nick's regulars.

"I'm fine. I can handle it." Even as I said the words, I knew they were a lie. I ran my hands over my hair, then growled. "I need to go."

"Are you going to go talk to your dad?" Nick asked, anger in his gaze.

"I will. When I see them. I need to go find Brooke first."

"Make sure she's safe," Sebastian said, his voice quiet.

"You want me to talk to one of my friends down at the precinct?" Jared asked.

"I'll figure something out."

"Leif," Nick said, the disappointment and anger in that one word evident.

I let out a breath, the clock ticking loudly in my head. "Fine, I should talk to the authorities. So they at least know he's harassing me. But I need to talk to Brooke."

"We can do that. Come on, I'll go with you," Jared said.

I shook my head. "No, I can do this."

"And I'm going with you," Nick said.

"Well, our tattoo artists are going, it looks like I'm coming, too," Brett put in.

"I'll stay here and hold down the fort." Sebastian put in.

"I'm taking up your days," I said, shame crawling up my spine.

"No, that man came in and harassed you, and from what it sounds like, he's probably on parole. So let's see what we can do to keep your family safe." Jared nodded tightly before getting his things.

"What the hell does he want from me?" I asked as Nick glared.

"He wants everything he couldn't have before because he's a bully. And I know all about bullies, Leif. We'll fix this. But you have to stop trying to handle it on your own. You have to stop trying to hide the stress from your family."

"I just don't want to hurt them," I said, my voice breaking.

"Then don't. But you're not going to get hurt because of that asshole. So come on. Let's go."

I let my best friend, and two men I hardly knew, walk me out the door and right back into my past.

It was my present that kept echoing in my head.

I needed to keep Brooke safe.

Even if I made the wrong choice in the end. The only choice I could.

Chapter 16

Brooke

"It always stuns me that I know a real, live, nuclear physicist," May stated as she sipped her drink.

I laughed as Lake clapped her hands. "Isn't she brilliant? I mean, she's a physicist, so I knew she was brilliant, but the way that she can casually just discuss radioactive materials, silicates, and chemical leaching without anyone the wiser just makes me grin."

"That was for my graduate degree. I don't work with that branch anymore. At least not in detail."

The girls went on to ask more questions about physics, and I did my best to answer them. I didn't do the same type of research I had back in California or even in graduate school. Instead, my research went in a slightly different direction. I wasn't a rocket scientist like Leif called me at one point, but I was close to it. At least in some aspects.

I ate a bite of my cupcake, then sipped my champagne as the three of us enjoyed our girl time. Luke snuggled into my side and I kissed the top of his head. He might not understand all of the physics explanations I was going into, but he enjoyed being part of the group. And I loved the fact that while I was slowly making friends, Luke was part of everything. He was my everything. I might be finding myself in a serious relationship with Leif, somehow slowly finding my footing at work again, but no matter what, Luke was mine. My everything.

"I want to be a tattoo artist," Luke said suddenly, and Lake gave me a knowing look.

Luke had been looking at Leif these days as if he were my little boy's hero, and I was a little worried about that. What happened when Leif left? When things didn't work out? It was hard to find the balance, and I wasn't sure I was doing it right.

"Do you want to show us what tattoo you would make? Your crayons are right here," I said, pointing towards the coffee table where Luke and May had played with coloring books earlier.

"Okay, Mommy," Luke said as he scrambled down off the couch and knelt in front of the coffee table.

He bit his lip, then tapped his chin with his pointer finger as he studied the crayons, and then reached for a blue one before starting his outline.

"You're going with blue?" I asked

"I need to sharpen the purple one because purple is what you outline with." He nodded tightly and then went back to his drawings.

I widened my gaze, trying to think when he would have learned something like that.

"I think I remembered Leif saying that he and Luke had talked about tattoos before when you were making dinner a couple of nights ago," Lake said, as if she had known where my brain had gone.

I nodded as May and Lake continued to speak, watching Luke draw.

I needed to sit down with my son and have a long conversation about what it meant for Mommy to be dating. He knew that Leif was my friend and was honestly so great with him.

I hadn't meant to begin a serious relationship before Leif, but this happy accident had turned into something I wanted to trust.

I just needed to learn to trust again.

We had dinner with his family coming up in a couple of days, and Luke was coming, too. It scared me to think that I was taking all these serious steps, but I felt like I was also just getting started. I had known Leif for longer than anyone else in the state. I was friends with his cousins, his family, and him.

And I trusted him.

"You look like you just had a revelation," Lake whispered as she leaned toward me.

May smiled over at me, winked, then looked down at Luke's drawing.

"I'm just thinking," I answered.

"About?" Lake prodded.

I looked over at the other woman as she tugged on her long sleeve. She had her hair piled up on the top of her head and was wearing foundation but no other makeup. It seemed out of place for her since Lake was usually so put together.

"The fact that I'm falling for your cousin," I whispered, barely more than a breath.

May heard, though, and gave me a thumbs-up as Lake clapped her hands.

"I knew it. I like to think that I had something to do with this, but knowing my cousin, he would always find a way into your life."

We were being quiet as we watched Luke draw.

"I just have to take things slow. Be careful."

Lake nodded. "Because you're a good person, and an even better mom."

I smiled at her as the doorbell rang and I frowned, wondering who it could be.

I got off the couch, waving May down, as she and Lake went to help Luke with his drawing, each of my friends adding their tattoos to the paper.

I looked through the peephole, and warmth spread through me, my toes curling as I opened the door to see Leif standing there.

He had his hands in his pockets as he rocked back, a serious expression on his face.

I studied his eyes, the darkness in them, and dread filled my stomach even as I told myself I was just reading too much into it.

He opened his mouth to speak and then shook his head as if he were trying to figure out what to say.

Alarmed, I stepped out on the porch, closing the door behind me. "What is it?" I asked.

"I don't think I can do this anymore," he said after a minute, shocking me. I pressed my back against the door, my eyes wide. "What? You can't do what anymore?"

He pulled his hand out of his pocket and gestured between the two of us. "This. It's not working out. I have to go. You're safer here."

"Safer? What the hell are you talking about? Are you breaking up with me out of the blue and not telling me why? What is going on, Leif?"

"It's over, Brooke. This was nice. But I can't do this."

Then he turned on his heel and left. That's when I realized that he hadn't even driven here. He'd walked from his place on the other side of the neighborhood, and I just stood there, shaking.

Lake opened the door after what seemed like an hour, or possibly ten minutes, and frowned. "I heard someone shout, but it wasn't my cousin, right? Why are you standing there? Why are you so pale?"

I turned at her, my eyes widening. "I have to go figure out what the hell just happened."

"What is wrong, Mommy?" Luke asked and my heart twisted.

I had just told myself that I was trusting Leif. That I was falling for him. And Leif showed up, leaving us, leaving Luke. Well damn it. I was not going to let that happen. No matter what, I would not let him hurt my son.

Or myself.

I moved past Lake to kneel in front of Luke. I pushed his hair away from his face, realizing he needed another haircut, and kissed his forehead. "I need to go talk to a friend. Do you think you can stay with May and Lake for a little bit? You can have another cupcake."

Yes, I was bribing my son, trying to make him feel

better because he could sense the nervousness wafting off me.

"I like cupcakes." Then he leaned forward and kissed the tip of my nose and I nearly burst into tears. "Don't be sad, Mommy. You'll fix it. You fix everything."

I knew my son had no idea what he was talking about, but I wanted to be that strong. To be the protector who could fix things. I just had no idea how I was going to fix this.

"What happened?" Lake asked, concern etched on her features.

I swallowed hard. "I think Leif just broke up with me." My voice broke, but I refused to cry. I did not have time to break down. I had to fix this and let my anger take over because I would be damned if Leif walked away like this. Not when something else had to be going on.

He had been the one to hold me, to get angry with me over what had happened at work. He had been the one to start this relationship with me when I wasn't sure I had the time or strength to do so. And yet he could just walk away?

Lake's eyes widened, and she nearly staggered back.

"Anything you need. We're here. Something must have happened because I saw the way he looks at you. He loves you."

My heart stopped for a moment, and everything went cold. "I don't know about that, but I thought he at least respected me enough to tell me what's on his mind."

May was watching us, but she kept her attention on Luke, and for that, I was grateful. They would take care of my son while I figured this out. I trusted them, and I had to believe in that trust. Because if I allowed myself to break down after just thinking I could trust Leif with everything, I was not going to make it for long.

I said goodbye to them, and since I'd had two glasses of wine, I walked toward Leif's house rather than getting behind the wheel.

It might be after dark, but the streetlights were on and there was a full moon. I would only need a few more minutes outside to make it to his place. I'd always found it comforting that we lived so close, even as I resisted starting a relationship, and yet he had just walked away. From me, from everything.

Damn it. I couldn't let him do this.

At least not without answers.

I stormed up to his porch and banged on the front door, ringing the doorbell a couple of times for good measure. The light in his living room was on, so he had to be home, even though his car was probably parked in the garage. We'd barely spent any time at his place, mainly because Luke had everything at my place. It was just easier.

Was that the problem? Was it because he felt like I wasn't taking this serious enough, putting enough effort in?

I swallowed hard, a single notion of worry sliding into anger. Maybe I didn't put in as much effort as I needed to. He was always the one setting up dates and taking me out when we had time. But the three of us did things together. Although not as much as Leif probably would like. I was taking things slow, trying not to hurt Luke or get his hopes up.

Or rather, my own hopes.

That was the truth. I didn't want to hurt myself, so maybe I had hurt Leif in the process.

Leif answered the door, his hair disheveled as if he'd been running his hands through it, his eyes wide. I'd only been a few minutes behind him, and yet he looked even worse now than he had on my porch. "Brooke? Why are you here?"

I ignored the knife in my heart at that and pushed past him.

"You better be alone in here and not cheating on me. Because if that's why you broke up with me, you will have to answer for a lot more."

Leif's eyes widened, the hurt on his face slicing into me. But I had to be numb. Had to ignore it. "There is no one else, Brooke. Why would you think that of me?"

"Why else? You broke up with me out of the blue. What else am I supposed to think? What is wrong?" I let out a breath, shaking. "What is *wrong*, Leif? Because you can't have had a personality change this drastic in the hours since we last spoke. What happened?"

"Nothing, everything. Brooke. It is better for you if I'm not around. Better for Luke."

"No, you don't get to bring up my son after walking away. You invited us to the damn farmers' market. You wanted us to go out and enjoy it as a family. Like a damn *family*, and here you are, walking away? You said it wasn't safe before. What do you mean by that? If you want to break up with me like this, I need answers. It's what I do for a living. Find answers. So give them to me. Now."

My voice rose with each sentence as I moved forward, pressing my finger against his chest. "Talk to me."

"Brooke," he said, his voice barely above a whisper.

"Tell me what's wrong. Don't walk away from me. You made me believe in you, Leif. Trust you. Don't break that trust. Don't break me."

Now I was crying, my anger bursting like a bubble as I just wanted to know why.

"It's to keep you safe," he said, pressing his forehead to mine.

"I'm going to need a better answer than that." My

hands shook and I stepped back, wiping away my tears as I stared at him. "I deserve better than that, Leif. And so do you. I left my son with Lake and May, and I walked here. I need to know what I did wrong."

I hadn't meant to say that, and my voice broke at the words. Leif cursed under his breath and began to pace. "You didn't do anything wrong. I promise you. I'm just trying to keep you safe."

I threw my hands in the air. "What do you mean by that? What on earth could I be in danger from? Just tell me. Tell me. I deserve that. You don't get to make my choices for me."

"Brooke, Roger threatened you."

I blinked at him, confused. "Roger?"

"Fuck. I need to start at the beginning."

"Yes. You do."

"You didn't do anything wrong. I promise you. I love being with you. I love seeing you and spending time with you. I love spending time with Luke. You coming back into my life the way you did changed everything. I would never take that for granted."

"You were just going to walk away without a second thought."

"There were a lot of thoughts, Brooke."

"Then tell me," I whispered, my voice breaking. "Tell me."

Leif met my gaze, the agony in his eyes breaking

me. "My birth mom had a lot of boyfriends when I was younger. You know that when she got pregnant, she hid it from my dad, Austin. She said it was because she thought she could be a better mom, that she and my birth dad weren't too close and so that's why she did it. And maybe my dad believes that. Or maybe he just hid his anger from losing ten years of my life for me so well. I don't know because all I remember is that my mom tried her best at the beginning and then quit trying. But when she started doing drugs, started dating men that hated her, and hit her, I had always thought, looking back on it, that she would've died from something else if she hadn't gotten sick."

I didn't have any words for this. I couldn't even imagine putting Luke in the situation Leif had been in, and my heart hurt. "I'm so sorry."

"I am, too. I know she tried sometimes, but not always. And while I told my therapist this, I didn't really tell my parents too much about it. I didn't want them to feel guilty about not being there for the first ten years of my life. And they *shouldn't* feel guilty. It wasn't my dad's fault that he didn't know I existed. The moment he knew I existed, he took me in. Sierra was barely even dating Austin at the time and took me in. They *are* my parents."

"And how is Roger connected?" I asked, confused, trying to keep up. I wanted to reach out and hold him, but he kept pacing, and I knew he needed space to tell me these things.

"He was my mom's boyfriend. My mom never married him. He went to jail before my mom died. So he wasn't even around when I was thrust into the system. They tried to figure out where I would go. I don't remember a lot of the legal part of that, about how hard my dad fought, or even if the will stated where custody went. I don't know the legal stuff. But the man my mother was dating before she died was a horrible person. He was in prison for a long time, longer than I ever thought possible, because of what he did while he was behind bars. But now he's out."

I looked up and then, my eyes wide. "When did he get out?"

"Right about the time you moved in. When we started to be together, he sent a threatening note. Because he wants money or to scare me like he did when I was a kid."

"Oh, Leif. I am so sorry. Why didn't you tell me this?" I asked.

He pushed his hair from his face, and I wanted to hold him and tell him everything was going to be okay. "I didn't want to worry you. I realize that that's stupid. The only people that know are Nick and Sebastian. One of the only reasons they even know is because Roger showed up."

"He showed up? At your house?"

He shook his head. "No, at Montgomery Ink Legacy. That's also where he sent the note. I don't think he knows where I live, but now that I've talked to the authorities, they are going to keep an eye on him. Roger is out on parole, so they will talk to his parole officer. But there's no real evidence other than him coming by. I don't have a restraining order against the man. Why would I?"

"Leif…I am so sorry."

He moved forward and cupped my face. I wanted to move away, unsure what I felt, but I didn't. He needed me just as much as I needed him. Maybe that realization told me that he had pushed me away for a reason. But we needed to be better than that.

"He came in today, and he threatened you and Luke. He saw you leaving my place, and he threatened you. I was going to tell you about that so that you could be on alert. The cops will want to talk to you, too. I had this whole speech planned out to tell you, then I saw you, and I heard Luke laughing, and I just needed to end it to keep you safe."

I push back, my eyes wild. "He threatened my son?"

Leif nodded. "Yes. I'm never going to let him hurt Luke. Or you. I'll do whatever I can."

"You were just going to walk away."

"To protect you."

I snarled. "That's idiotic. If he's going to threaten

us, he will do so even if we are no longer together. Nobody hurts my son, Leif."

"Damn straight. Nobody will hurt you or your son."

"No one will hurt you either, damn it," I practically screamed. "Don't hurt *us* by walking away."

"The authorities are going to talk to you tomorrow. I promise you I was going to tell you everything. Only I saw you, and everything went blank. I wanted to keep you safe. So I ran."

"That's stupid," I blurted.

Leif raised his brows. "What?"

"That's stupid. No, you don't get to break up with me. I didn't break up with you, and you acted like the alpha asshole after my attack. We will work through this together because if someone is threatening you, then we need to keep *you* safe. You will tell the girls and your family about what's going on, so everybody is safe. Keeping this all bundled up and trying to take care of everything by yourself doesn't work. No one is going to hurt this family. But you need to tell me when you're in pain, or when you're scared. Because I don't know how to keep us safe if you don't tell me things."

He leaned forward and kissed me then, hard and fast, before he stepped away, breathing hard. "Brooke."

"Tell everyone. But don't leave me." I hadn't meant to say that. I pressed my lips together, annoyed that I'd once again left myself so open. When he nodded tightly and kissed me again, my thoughts began to whirl.

It was hard to think with Leif Montgomery around.

"I just wanted to keep you safe."

"Then be by my side and do it. Be open. No more secrets."

"I'm sorry. I'm sorry for hurting you. For acting like an idiot."

He kissed me again, and I stepped away as my phone buzzed.

"I'm sorry for yelling back at you. One second."

Lake: *Everything okay?*

I looked up at Leif, at the hunger and seriousness in his gaze, and swallowed hard. I needed him. I knew we needed to talk more. But right then? I needed him.

Me: *Yes. Finally. Give me an hour?*

Lake: **smiley emoji* Take your time. We've got Luke. And cupcakes.*

I laughed, then set my phone on the table beside me.

"Since you scared me, I think it's time you make it up to me." Leif's eyes widened for a minute before he grinned.

"Oh, I think I can do that."

And then his lips were on me, and I sighed, wrapping my arms around his neck.

He gripped my ass, then lifted me. I wrapped my

legs around his hips, continuing to kiss him as we thrust against one another. And then he was walking, taking me to the dining room.

"Leif?"

"There is something that I've wanted to do for a while now."

He set me on the dining room table and then slid his hands over my body and then up my chest, caressing my breasts before cupping my face again.

"I will never hurt you again."

"Just talk to me. That's all we need."

"I think I might give you a little more than that," he said with a wink, and then my shirt was over my head and his lips were on my breasts.

I tried to keep up, tried not to breathe too quickly or to make too many moaning sounds. But it was hard to focus on anything for too long when he was there, touching me, kissing me. Then my bra was off, and he was pulling at my leggings.

Somehow, I was ripping off his clothes, and then we were both naked in his dining room. He knelt in front of me, my legs spread wide.

"Hands on the table, keep your legs spread."

"Leif."

"Now, Brooke," he ordered, and then he was licking me, sucking on my clit, spreading my lower folds. I groaned, riding his face as he continued to suck and lick and eat me out right on the dining table.

He hummed along my clit before he twisted his lips slightly, and I came, my body going tight and then relaxed against his face. He licked, and he sucked, and then he moved back, licking my juices from his lips. His beard was wet, and I wanted to blush, but I couldn't, not with all the heat and warmth sending shockwaves through my body.

He gripped his cock, slid his thumb over the piercing at the end. Then he thrust into his palm before I finally gathered my strength and slithered down the table to my knees. I gripped his thighs, digging my nails into his skin, and he smiled down at me, sliding his hand through my hair.

"Look at you on your knees in front of me. I like that look."

I spread my thighs and slid my hand between my legs, sliding over my swollen clit. "I want you."

"I'm going to come right on those pretty breasts if you keep touching yourself like that."

I grinned before I took him in one hand and swallowed him whole. He hit the back of my throat and groaned. He tugged on my hair and I swallowed, my throat closing around the tip of his dick.

I continued to play with myself, sliding my fingers in and out of my wet heat as I bobbed along his cock, hollowing my throat as I relaxed, letting him slide down deeper.

He thrust his hips, practically fucking my face as I did the same with my fingers. I knew I was wet, literally dripping on the floor, as he pulled back and then gripped me again. Somehow, I was in his arms, wrapped around him, his cock sliding between my folds and over my stomach as he moved me to the table again. He set my feet on the floor then twisted me, putting my ass in the air as he slid his length between my cheeks.

"I need a condom," he whispered before pressing a quick kiss to my shoulder and moving to the other side of the room. I kept playing with myself, moaning, before he came back and slid right into me in one thrust.

I could barely breathe, standing on my tiptoes, as he began to work in and out of me, hard, fast, needy.

When he slid his finger along my ass, spreading me, playing with me in a way he hadn't before, I groaned and moved so he could go deeper.

"That's my girl. My dirty, dirty girl."

"Make me come already," I ordered, my voice low, throaty.

He laughed roughly before he slid his hands over my breasts and then in my hair, pulling me back for a deep kiss that sent me over the edge.

I came over him, shaking, my knees going weak as he came too, holding me close.

Somehow we were both on the floor, wrapped in

one another as we continued to move through our orgasms.

I couldn't breathe, couldn't think.

But this was Leif. He was taking care of me, even though was hard and fast, it was what we both needed.

And I made a vow right then and there.

I would never let anyone hurt him.

Not even myself.

Chapter 17

Brooke

"DON'T BE NERVOUS. YOU KNOW THEM ALREADY. YOU don't have to be scared."

I narrowed my gaze at Leif. "So says the man who is about to take me to a Montgomery family dinner, as if it's not a daunting task."

"It's not going to be too daunting. I promise you."

"I'm excited. Will there be cheese?" Luke asked, and my lips twitched as Leif took a staggered step back, his hand over his chest. "Will there be cheese? It's like you don't even know me, kid. Of course, there's going to be cheese. It's a Montgomery dinner."

"What if somebody doesn't like cheese comes to visit, would they be kicked out?"

Leif lifted Luke into his arms as my son began to laugh, and I ignored that little clutch of my belly at the sight. We were walking up the long driveway to Austin and Sierra's house, and from the cars already parked in the driveway, we were possibly the last ones there.

I didn't like being late, but I'd had a morning meeting with a few advisors that hadn't been able to be postponed. Leif understood, and he told me his family would as well, but I still felt bad about it.

"If someone does not like cheese, then they are forever ostracized."

"What does ostrich-sized mean?"

"What that means it's a big bird," Leif said, laughing at his own joke as I rolled my eyes. "But ostracize means that they are forever kicked out of the family." At Luke's wide eyes, Leif tapped Luke on the nose. "But I was only kidding. If somebody doesn't like cheese, that just means more cheese for us. However, if you bring in any processed or fake cheese into the house, you are forever gone. That is a fon-don't, not a fondue. It must be gouda to be good."

I rolled my eyes. "How many cheese jokes do you have for this?"

"I have amassed a countless supply of cheese, dairy, and cow jokes from a long life of cheese-related humor. Just know that this will not be the first time you hear them, nor the last. It's sort of what you're forced into since you're with me."

He took my hand and my heart sped. Here I was, meeting the family, about to go to an actual dinner, and bringing my son. This was a big step. A scary one.

Leif's parents lived less than twenty minutes away, in the suburb just north of ours. They had a large house that I knew was Montgomery built. It was a two-story place with beautiful corbels under the eaves.

It looked like a home, welcoming, and with the backdrop of the Rocky Mountains, it was gorgeous. Leif told me that there was a huge deck on the back, one where he and his family had eaten countless dinners. Tonight, we would be eating inside since the mosquitoes were terrible.

"This home is beautiful. It's like something out of my childhood dreams."

"Well, that's a nice thing to hear when I walk outside," Sierra said as she opened the door and beamed at me.

I blushed, not having realized that she was there. "Oh, well, I love the house."

"So do I. Austin had it built before we were married, and I moved in and never left. We have done some renovations to keep it updated and the like, but the Montgomerys know how to build."

"That's what I like to hear," Austin said as he came up behind Sierra and put his hand on her shoulder. He was a full head taller than her, his big beard flecked with slight to moderate granite. They looked happy and in love and as if they had been made for each other.

That was what I wanted. That settled happiness still seemed to thrive even after four children and countless changes. Could I have that with Leif? I wasn't sure. I wasn't sure if I could trust myself enough for that, but maybe I should try.

Luke scrambled down out of Leif's hold and practically ran toward Sierra.

My eyes widened as Leif's mom bent down and lifted Luke up to her waist.

"Hello there," she said, laughing.

"It is good to see you again. Thank you for welcoming us into your home." Luke said it slowly, reciting everything I had told him, and Sierra beamed as Austin rubbed his mouth, holding back a smile.

"We're trying," Leif said, and once again, my heart did that pit-pat thing.

Because he said *we*.

We were trying. Together.

I was in love with Leif Montgomery, and I needed to come to terms with that.

"Come on inside. We'll get you all situated with the Montgomerys," Austin said as Sierra moved into the house, Luke in her arms as the two of them talked.

I bit my lip, walked inside, and handed over the bottle of wine I had brought.

"Like Luke said, thank you for welcoming us into your home."

"Thank you for bringing this stranger with you, since I never get to see him these days." Austin took the bottle from my hand and then held me close, giving me a big bear hug.

I swallowed hard, tears stinging my eyes.

What was with me?

Leif hugged his dad and then gestured towards the living room.

"And here is the rest of my immediate family. There's Colin." He pointed to a tall man with dark hair and thick-rimmed glasses perched on the bridge of his nose. I knew that Colin was finishing up his last year of college. He grinned as he came toward us.

"Finally, the woman that tamed the beast."

"Colin," Leif growled, but Leif's little brother waved him off, picked me up around the waist and twirled me around the living room.

"Welcome to the Montgomerys."

I sputtered and laughed. "He said you were going to be the one that made a scene."

"At least I'm living up to my expectation."

"Okay, hands off my woman," Leif growled as he pulled me back.

"Seriously? You decide to go with *my woman?*" I asked, laughing.

"I've got to claim my territory. There are a lot of freaking Montgomerys out there. This is why it's just the immediate family today, rather than all of the cousins and aunts and uncles. I don't think you're ready for that kind of dinner."

"Nobody is," a young woman said from the couch as she stood up, her twin brother beside her.

"Gideon, Jamie, this is Brooke. And over there, in Mom's arms, is Luke." My son waved from Sierra's arms, and I had to wonder if I was ever going to hold my son again tonight, because he looked mighty comfortable in Sierra's arms. Of course, that just made me smile.

"It's nice to meet you," Gideon said, grinning. "Will you drive us around? Or let us drive your car?"

"Gideon Montgomery," Austin growled, though I could hear the laughter in his tone.

"What am I missing?" I asked as Leif pinched the bridge of his nose.

"The twins are trying to get their driver's licenses, which means they need adults who are suckers enough to let them drive their cars. Do not touch Brooke's car. She has Luke to drive around, so if you wreck it, then Luke won't have a car."

"Well, that's a leap of logic," Jamie said with a

teenage roll of her eyes. "We'll be careful, and it is not like Luke would be in the car as we drove."

I held up my hands in surrender. "I'm not getting in the middle of this, but I bet you Leif could help. He is the big brother, and he's nice."

"Brooke," he growled, but his eyes were filled with laughter.

"Oh, we already like you. You're going to fit nicely," Austin said as he squeezed my shoulders and led me to the sitting room.

"We all helped cook, so Sierra didn't have to do it all on her own, but she's still the best cook of us all."

"I'm catching up," Colin said, his chin raised.

"Yes, you are," Sierra said, grinning. "Now, what can we get you to drink?"

"Milk?" Luke asked as he came practically barreling towards my legs.

I laughed, thankful that Leif kept me standing upright.

"We do have milk, as long as it's okay with your mom," Sierra answered.

I nodded. "Milk is good, but you also need to have water. Okay?"

"Okay."

"Come on. I have the perfect cup for you. It used to be Leif's. I don't throw anything away."

Austin rolled his eyes, much as his teenage daughter had. "I don't know why she said that. She's constantly cleaning out the house so we don't end up like hoarders." he grumbled.

"Let me guess. She finally threw away those old shorts that were more holes than cloth." Leif grinned.

"They were fine."

"Dad, you used to have to wear shorts underneath them so you didn't get arrested for indecent exposure." Jamie added with a huff, her eyes dancing.

Austin growled though it was halfhearted. "I swear, I'm outnumbered by all of you."

"I don't know. I seem to be the one surrounded by Montgomerys. I think Luke and I are the ones outnumbered."

"Okay, fine. I guess that counts." Austin winked. "Come on, let's get you that drink, now that Luke is taken care of."

Soon, I found myself laughing over barbecue ribs and fajitas, two foods that Leif loved, and they hadn't been able to choose which one to eat. There was pico de gallo and cilantro, beans and a fruit salad, macaroni and cheese, and coleslaw. Somehow it was the perfect amount of food for everybody though, without anyone feeling like they had to overeat. Everything was delicious, and I knew I needed a recipe or two for the sauce at least.

"Are these tortillas homemade?" I asked, after Luke and I shared a final one.

Sierra grinned. "Yes, one of my nieces went down

to San Antonio for school for a while and learned how to make them from her roommate's family."

"I'm jealous."

"I can teach you. It's fun. I bet Luke would have fun making them, too."

Luke grinned, his mouth closed but full of tortilla.

"I'm going to take that as a yes," I said with a laugh.

"I know you only wanted immediate family here," Austin said after a moment, looking at Leif. "But I wanted to invite Lake, as I need to meet this man of hers."

"You know, I haven't met Zach either," I said with a frown. "That's weird, right?"

"They are both constantly out of town, and when they are in town, they want to spend time together. I guess it makes sense." Leif said as he shrugged. "I met him on that double date. Remember?"

"Oh yes, when you went on a date with my nanny," I teased.

The table broke out into laughs and hoots as Luke's eyes widened.

"You and May?"

"I just went out to dinner with May. She's nice. But you know, I have a thing for your mom."

Everybody laughed louder as I shook my head, blushing.

"Of course you like Mom. She's the best," Luke

said, as if that was everything in the world, and went back to his tortilla.

"Well then," Austin said, clearing his throat even though he was still laughing. "I still want to meet him. I know that my cousin Liam, Lake's father, can handle it, but since she lives near us, I feel a sense of responsibility for my generation."

"I'm sure Lake can handle everything on her own," Sierra said, admonishing her husband. "But if we happen to invite her over for dinner just because, maybe with a few of the nieces, she can bring her boyfriend. Then we can meet him and interrogate him."

"I'm going to have to take notes on how you think," I said with a laugh.

"Before you know it, your kids are asking to go to school dances, go on dates, to drive. Then it's college, starting their own business, and bringing home a lovely woman that we adore, along with her amazing son." Sierra winked, and I blushed even harder as Leif let out a sigh.

"Subtle, Mom."

"You know I try."

"Speaking of dates, we saw Sebastian and Marley out at the Connolly Brewery for dinner yesterday."

I turned to the twins, frowning. "Marley is Sebastian's girlfriend, right?" I asked.

"Yep, and I keep waiting for him to propose

already," Jamie said, that teenage winsome note in her voice.

"They're too young to get married," Sierra said before she stiffened. "Great, now I sound like an uppity mother from a TV show. But they are only eighteen."

"Sebastian's nearly nineteen," Leif corrected.

"And they do love each other. I just still think of them as babies. And that's on me." She narrowed her eyes at the twins. "You two are fifteen. So don't even start thinking about it."

"I'm just saying they're adorable," Jamie said.

"Don't worry. I'm looking to get married once I'm old, like thirty." Gideon grinned as he said it, and Leif rolled his eyes.

"You're lucky there's a kid here."

"You are lucky that I'm here," Luke said as he beamed, and I cackled, the rest joining me.

By the time we cleaned up and headed out to the porch for the evening, Leif cleared his throat and whispered something to Jamie. She gave him an odd look and then nodded before holding out her hand.

"Hey, Luke, do you want to see our playroom? It's changed over the years, but there might be a couple of toys to show you."

Gideon stepped right up as if the twins had mind-reading abilities. "Yeah, come on, kiddo."

Luke looked at me and I nodded, knowing why

Leif wanted Luke out of the room along with his youngest siblings.

The three walked away, and Austin gave us a worried look before clearing his throat. "What is it that you want to tell us that you didn't want little ears around for?" he asked, his voice soft.

Colin, I noticed, had been allowed to stay, but considering he was an adult, that made sense. Sierra slid her hand into Austin's while I did the same to Leif's.

"I have to tell you something, and you're going to get mad, but let me get through it."

I squeezed his hand again, and Leif let out a breath before explaining the entire situation about Roger.

As expected, Austin growled and threw his hands in the air. "Why the hell didn't you tell us?"

"Austin, let him finish," Sierra put in, even as she glared at her son. "Once you're finished, then we can yell at you."

"Damn straight," Colin added.

Leif ran his hand through his hair and went through every detail, sparing no feelings, and even mentioned how he had broken up with me for those few short minutes.

Colin reached out and smacked the back of Leif's head, but nobody admonished him for it. Instead, they continued to listen to Leif. When he finished, I hugged him tightly and moved back so Sierra could hold her son. Colin began to rant, repeatedly going over what happened and asking questions. Leif answered systematically, and I knew this was hard for him.

Then Austin spoke, and everyone quieted. "All this time. All this fucking time, Leif. You never told me. I don't know why."

Because Sierra was holding her son, Colin came up to me and hugged me tightly. It was as if I was part of the family already, and tears slid down my cheeks. I looked over and saw Sierra was crying, too.

Austin sighed. "I wish you would've told me all those years ago about everything that happened to you. I thought I knew, I thought you would have told me, but you didn't. We're going to have to work through that, but the thing is…we're family, Leif."

"I know that, Dad, I promise you. I'm sorry."

"We're a family, meaning we're going to handle this together. I know you thought you had to handle this on your own because you're the oldest and because you feel like everybody is trying to lean on you. We talked about this. We've all got you. People younger than you, older than you, all of us. So, we're going to deal with this as a family." Austin Montgomery looked at me then, his eyes directly on mine. "And that means you too, Brooke. You and Luke. We're all a family in this. So we will protect each other, and we will keep that man out of our lives. Just like we should've done all those years ago. Come here, son," Austin growled as he moved forward and opened his arms. Leif went straight into them, as did Sierra. Colin tugged on me, and suddenly the five of us were hugging, laughing, and crying.

In that moment, I knew I truly loved Leif. His family loved him so much that while they were angry that he had hidden this, they loved him more than that anger. They cared for him and wanted to keep him safe. And they wanted to keep my son safe.

I had fallen in love with Leif Montgomery.

And I was truly scared I could lose him if we didn't protect him.

But right then and there, I let the Montgomerys hold me, and I imagined what it would mean to have a family like this.

And what it could mean if this was truly mine.

Chapter 18

Leif

"I HEAR THAT THE MEETING OF THE PARENTS WENT well," Sebastian said as he leaned against the wall.

I sipped my beer and nodded. "Brooke's met them a couple of times now, but dinner? Yeah, it went well."

Everybody in this room already knew about Roger and the threats. The authorities knew, so there was nothing to do other than be on alert and try to live our lives.

Brooke was at home grading papers and having Luke time. She had almost finished by the time I had left after dinner, and now she just wanted time alone with her son. If I hadn't had this guys' night already planned, I would've been able to stay as well. As if we were a family.

That hit me like a ton of bricks to the chest and I swallowed hard, thinking about us as a family. I had almost run because I was too scared.

I was still worried about what Roger would do. He thought I had money that I didn't have, or maybe he just wanted retribution for being in jail when I had my own life, but I had nothing to do with that. And maybe once the man understood that, or once the cops talked to him, things would be better.

Until that happened, the doors were locked, Brooke was behind the security system that my family's company had put in, and I was trying not to be over-whelmed by the fact that they were being threatened because of my past. A past that had nothing directly to do with me, but that didn't help me sleep at night.

"Earth to Leif. What's up with you?" Leo asked.

I looked at my fellow tattoo artist, then Tristan, Nick, and Sebastian, and tried my best to push away all thoughts of the man who haunted my nightmares and focus on what was in front of me.

"Sorry, just thinking."

"You better not be thinking about that asshole," Nick warned, ever the best friend.

"If it helps, my thoughts started with Brooke."

"That's always good," Leo said, grinning. "She seems nice... You know, I'm real nice. She have a sister? It would be killer to find a woman who doesn't mind the ink and my job."

"She doesn't have a sister, but I know you can find someone. I didn't realize you were looking." I took another sip of my beer.

"I don't know if I'm looking for forever actively, but I'm not *not* looking."

Tristan rolled his eyes. "What my cohort over here is saying is that love looks good on you."

Everyone was silent for a minute when I didn't spit out my beer, and Nick's eyes widened. "Well then. *Love.* Does Brooke know that?"

I shrugged and played with the label on my bottle. "Probably. I just haven't actually told her."

"You know, as the resident love expert here, I do have to say telling her is the first step. The most important step. Just like we men joke that we can't read women's minds. They, in turn, cannot read ours."

Both Tristan and Leo glared at Sebastian while Nick and I burst out laughing.

"The thing is, of all of us, the hatchling knows what he's talking about. It is not even a little contrived."

Sebastian shrugged, though there was something in his eyes I couldn't quite read. "I may be young, but I know things. I have responsibilities. And I know I love Marley. That's all that matters, you know?"

"I know," I said. I cleared my throat. "I'm going to tell her. I just don't know how to do it."

"Start with the words," Nick said with a shrug. "What do I know? I'm not in a serious relationship. Not like the kid here."

"Excuse me. I'm your business partner, not just a kid." Sebastian raised his chin, his eyes filled with laughter.

"That is true. But until you can buy me a beer, I don't know if I can stop making fun of you."

"So, is that the age that you finally treat me like a grown-up?" he teased.

"No, I'll just keep moving the finish line. Then it will be renting a car. And then the age where we have to go to bed early because life sucks. Which is thirty, by the way," Nick added.

"You're not kidding about the whole thirty thing. I thought people were joking when they said once you turn thirty, your body starts to give out, but I was picking up Luke the other day, and my back twinged." I shook my head in disgust as everybody else jeered. "I would be annoyed that you're laughing at me about my sad state of affairs, but honestly, I'm not an old man or anything, but I am thirty now. I guess this means I should start taking control of what I want."

"Hear hear," Leo put in. "Tell that woman that you love her. That you want to be with her and that Luke means everything in the world to you. Do it all. Then tell us exactly how to do it so I can take notes for when I find my lady love."

"Okay, first off, don't use the term 'lady love,'" Tristan said with a laugh.

Nick smiled. "Ever, seriously. And more power to both of you for finding relationships and making them work. When I get to your age, though? I don't see me falling like the rest of you. No, thank you. Relationships aren't worth the headache. I'm good just like I am. Getting Montgomery Ink Legacy off the ground, making sure Leif doesn't make any more stupid decisions, watching all of you Montgomerys and friends fall. That's not for me."

"Well, doesn't that sound like a challenge," Leo mumbled, and I held back a smile. No, I didn't think my best friend would appreciate me grinning just then, even though it did indeed sound like a challenge to the gods of fate.

Although I had eaten dinner earlier, I still had a couple of wings that Sebastian had brought over, saying he had a nervous stomach, and I just sighed at the eighteen, nearly nineteen-year-old who could gorge himself on wings and root beer as if he wasn't going to have heartburn later.

Leo and Tristan headed out, having dates, which I found ironic considering that Leo wanted me to hook him up with someone. He was going to have to slow down on the serial dating if he wanted something serious, but I wasn't going to be the one to tell him that. It had taken me long enough to figure it out.

Nick headed out next, saying he had an early morning, and left it at that. Knowing how Nick was growly over the idea of dating, I figured he was actually going home, but I didn't pressure him to say anything more.

That left Sebastian and me, and I knew he would be heading out soon because he had exams coming up, and I wanted to get back to Brooke. Although I had guys' night tonight, I would be spending the night in her bed. Exactly where I needed to be. It still surprised me how quickly everything had changed. I was going to stop trying to look for every fault there was.

"Hey, do you have a minute?" Sebastian asked as we were cleaning up the last of the dishes.

I frowned at the worried note in Sebastian's voice and nodded.

"Of course. What's up?" I asked, sliding the final plate into the dishwasher.

"I don't know how to start."

Tension slid up my spine and I swallowed hard, reaching out to grip Sebastian's shoulder. "Anything you have to say to me will stay between us. You know that's always the case with us. We're cousins. Family. Although, wait." I paused. "Except for Brooke. I feel weird about keeping secrets from her."

Sebastian's eyes widened, then he nodded. "Yeah,

you're right. I wouldn't keep secrets from Marley, especially after everything that just happened with Brooke. You shouldn't keep secrets from her." He let out a breath. "Hell. I should just say it."

My eyes widened. "Did you ask Marley to marry you? Is that what you're worried about? Because you know your parents love her. We all might think you guys are young, but you guys have been together forever."

Sebastian shook his head. "No, it's not that. I mean, I am going to marry Marley. I love her. She is my future. I know that. Damn it." He cursed a few more times, then looked me straight in the eyes. "Marley is pregnant."

I nearly dropped when I was holding and stared at my cousin. My teenage cousin. He might be an adult, might pay his own way, might soon own part of the business. He was in college and going towards his future.

But he was still only nearly nineteen.

"I don't know what to say."

Sebastian ran his hand through his hair, then began to pace through my kitchen. "We didn't mean for this to happen. She was on birth control until her parents found out, and yes, she's an adult, but her dad kept throwing it away. So we used a condom. Every time. We even used spermicide, and anything else we could've possibly done with her not being on birth control."

"Hold on. Her dad threw away her birth control?" I asked, practically shouting.

Sebastian held up his hand. "Her parents are ultra-conservative. To the point that they didn't even want her dating me. I thought I had won them over. But it didn't matter that Marley was in college, nearly nineteen. They didn't want their daughter to have sex, so they didn't let her have birth control. In their mind, that made sense. She was just getting on a new prescription, and she was going to hide it at my house when, well, apparently, condoms aren't one hundred percent effective."

My mind went in a thousand different directions as I tried to catch up. "I have so much to say to that. To begin with, I'm so sorry for Marley. For what her parents did because I feel like that's illegal."

Sebastian shook his head. "I don't know. *I don't know.* But it doesn't matter, does it? It's not like I can go back and add birth control. We never had a condom break, not to my knowledge, and were very careful. We've always been careful. There wasn't one slip up, one accidental 'oh, we can go back and fix it.' We were always careful. But she's pregnant. Marley is pregnant. We're going to keep it."

I reached forward and gripped his shoulders. "Okay. What do you need from me?" I asked softly.

Sebastian relaxed marginally before he pulled away and swallowed hard. "I'm an adult. I'm going to tell Mom and Dad. Because they deserve to know, because somehow my parents will be grandparents, and I have no idea how that's going to go."

I blinked and held back a laugh even though nothing was funny about the situation. But Grandpa Alex and Grandma Tabby had a certain ring to it.

"Her parents are not going to be okay with this. I don't know what they're going to do, but I'm going to take responsibility, and so will Marley. If we have to get married, we'll get married early. I know everyone joked that we were going to get married young, but we were going to wait till after college. We had *plans*. And this throws a wrench in it, but I don't want Marley to have to quit school. I don't want to quit school, either. I don't know. I just need to figure things out."

"I'm here when you need me. And you're going to need me. You'll need all of us. But that's what we Montgomerys do. We take care of each other. I know this is unexpected and so not the right time, but it's okay. We're going to figure this out. You and Marley are not alone." Then I smiled, even though my stomach twisted at the thought of my baby cousin being a dad. "Well then, Daddy. It looks like you have to learn how to change diapers," I teased.

Sebastian cursed under his breath before he

laughed, though I didn't hear much humor in it. "I'm so not ready for this."

"I don't think you're supposed to be ready for parenthood. Even when you think you will be. So you'll figure it out. Hell, you guys are helping me figure out how to keep Brooke and Luke safe. So, we will help you and Marley. You are not alone. You don't get kicked out of our family for having sex and dealing with the consequences. And now I feel like a jerk for calling a baby a consequence."

"I'm pretty sure I nearly did." Sebastian let out a breath. "I can figure something out. I don't know. But I just don't want Marley to be scared. Or feel like she's alone. Because her parents? They're not going to be understanding about this."

From the way that her parents sounded, no, I didn't think they were going to be understanding about it at all. And while I knew with certainty that every single one of our family members would understand, some would still grumble at the thought because it was a scary and monumental event.

I calmed Sebastian down a bit and then made sure he headed home. He would talk with his family in the morning, and then the rest of the Montgomerys would hear about it soon and be on board to do what they could. I just had to hope that in all of our numbers, we would be enough to help when Marley's parents made things difficult.

And from how Sebastian sounded, the fear he had, I had a feeling that was an actual worry.

I packed up my things and headed to Brooke's, wondering what else would change. Because Lake seemed to be in a serious relationship, Sebastian was about to be a dad, and here I was, finding myself with a seemingly ready-made family. It was scary as hell, and yet, I was ready for this. Scared but ready.

I knocked on Brooke's front door as I got there, and she opened it quickly, a smile on her face. "I saw you pull up. Would it be weird if I gave you a key?" she asked, tumbling over her words.

I grinned, my heart squeezing. "I was thinking I should give you a key to my place."

"Oh? That would be nice. Though I feel bad that we always do things at our house because Luke's here, and all his things are here. But then I end up feeling Luke and I are taking advantage of you."

I shook my head. "You are not. I like your place. And you're right, Luke's things are here."

"Maybe we can do better about taking turns. I don't know, but we can try."

I smiled. I leaned down and took her lips with mine. She groaned and I smiled, setting my bag down near the front door. "We can do whatever you want. I'm easy. A key sounds good, though. It would make things easier to help out around here more."

"Oh?" The fire flared back into her voice.

"Only because I want to. You were just saying that you needed somebody to help with the air filter because you can't reach it, even on a ladder. I'm a foot taller than you. I can help."

"I can reach if I jump," she said with a laugh.

"It's like we were both just now saying, you don't have to do things on your own, and we can try to help each other out. You have been doing most of the cooking because you like it, but I can help with other things. I don't know, Brooke. I'll be honest. I've never had a serious relationship like this before. I'm not good at it. So you're going to have to be patient with me as I figure out what we're supposed to do."

"I'm going to try to accept help. You're going to try to figure out what we're supposed to do. Because I don't know about serious relationships either, remember? I'm just as lost as you."

I raised a brow. "I didn't use the word lost."

She rolled her eyes and then led me back to the house as we tiptoed past Luke's room. "You didn't have to use the word. I got it in context."

I smiled and followed her back to her bedroom.

"Did you get your work done?" I asked as we got ready for the night. I didn't comment that this felt more like we were living together, a married couple, than anything I had ever felt in my life, because I didn't want to scare her away. But, hell, I was pretty scared too.

She piled her hair on the top of her head and then headed to her closet, probably to change into her pajamas.

I shrugged and then stripped down, keeping on my boxer shorts. Neither one of us slept naked in case Luke came in, though I had noticed that Brooke had locked the door.

She only locked the door if we wanted to keep Luke out.

And that was only for a certain reason.

My cock pressed through my boxer briefs, and I looked down, groaning. "Behave."

The door opened, and Brooke stood in short shorts and a tank top that barely held her generous breasts.

"Or don't behave." I blinked.

"Our faces are washed, your beard is clean, our teeth are brushed. I guess you just want to go and read in bed."

"Maybe. But it has been a long day. And I could use some tension relief." In more ways than one, I stood at attention. I swallowed hard. And then I was moving, cupping her face, and crushing my mouth to hers.

She tasted of mint and Brooke.

My dick slid against her belly and I licked her lips, then mine, before thrusting slightly against her.

"Those boxer briefs do not contain you at all," she teased, sliding her hand between us to squeeze.

My eyes nearly crossed and I groaned before picking her up and carrying her to the bedroom. She wrapped her arms around my neck as she held back a squeal.

"We have to be quiet. Luke will be able to hear us."

"I'm just saying if one of us wants to do some renovations to either one of our homes, soundproofing this bedroom will have to be number one." I tossed her on the bed, and she bounced, laughing.

"Oh, that was so sexy." She rolled her eyes, and I fell that much more in love.

Then I was over her, taking her shorts down, my mouth on her cunt before she could take her next breath. She put her hand over her mouth and arched, cupping her breast with her free hand as I licked her, spreading her, tasting her.

She was sweet and tart and everything that I craved. I was practically humping the bed as I went down on her, eating her out.

She came on my mouth in a silent scream, wet and hot and nearly sending me over the edge. We moved quickly, stripping each other, knowing each other more now than we ever had before. We had been hot and heavy all those years ago in Paris. We had quickly learned each other's bodies then.

But it was nothing like now. Our bodies had changed, we had changed, but this moment? We were more together now than we ever had been before.

When she rose above me and slid down, over my length, both of us groaned.

She rode me, cupping herself as I played with her nipples and her clit, both of us taking our time, knowing that even though the world might come down around us soon, this was our moment. And when she came, she clamped down around me, and I pulled her by her hair to my mouth. I took her mouth, kissing her hard, before I slid out of her and moved just as she was pressed against the bed. I pulled her hips, ass in the air, before I pounded into her, both of us groaning, trying to be quiet.

But there was nothing quiet about the heavy breaths, the sound of flesh against flesh, heat against heat.

And then I came, filling the condom, as I held back my groan.

I loved this woman.

I didn't want to wait any longer.

While still in her, I lay down behind her, holding her close.

"I love you, Brooke. I've loved you for far longer than this moment. But I can't hold it back anymore."

Brooke stiffened, and I was afraid I'd said the wrong thing. She looked over her shoulder, tears sliding down her cheeks.

"I love you, too, Leif. Now turn me around so I can see your face."

I laughed softly before I slid out of her, careful with the condom before I kissed her again.

"I love you," I whispered. I kissed her lips, a sweet touch of promise. "I love you."

"Love you, too."

She held me, and I knew that, no matter what happened next, no matter who came at us, no matter what pressures came forward, I loved Brooke.

She was mine. And I couldn't wait to tell the world.

Chapter 19

Brooke

I SLID OUT OF MY LAB COAT AND HEADED OUT OF THE lab, waving at my students as they finished up their work. I started early that morning, far earlier than I usually did, because I wanted to head home and meet with Leif and Luke for dinner. It was nice thinking that I had someone to come home to. It was a whole other dynamic that I was still getting used to.

I walked down the hallway towards my office and rolled my shoulders back, letting out a breath.

In the weeks since the attack, I had spoken with my therapist, the school board, and countless other administrative people. Honestly, I was tired of the politics behind it because everybody was so afraid that I would sue the school.

I just wanted to get past it, to get over it.

Because while they had created the environment that Landon had thrived in, nobody else had hurt me.

His father wasn't the president of the University anymore. The old guard would soon be leaving. The new guard consisted of people who trusted women, and my team were all people who were going to be safe because of the faculty in place.

Nobody had ever treated me like Landon had. In fact, everybody had always treated me with respect. And had continued to do so.

After the incident, I'd been afraid that they would think differently of me because I hadn't been strong enough to fend off the attack. But I had been. I'd gotten out of the office and called for help, and people had come to me. Nobody had taken Landon's side or blamed me.

Every single person believed me and had pushed Landon back.

The physics department at our university trusted women. They trusted who we were as scientists and people.

"You're looking introspective today," Patrice said as she came out of her office, books in tow.

"I was just thinking that our department is strong.

And worthy. I guess." I rolled my eyes at my words, but Patrice grinned.

"You're right. When I first started at the university, it was a boys' club with nearly no women. Now there are more and more coming every year. We are a diverse group, and we are brilliant. All of us."

I laughed, even though I believed her. "We are brilliant."

"I don't talk about my personal life often, mostly because it's not anybody's business, but I admire you, Brooke."

I froze, looking at the other woman who was slowly becoming my friend.

"When I first started here, I was a young academic, who eventually became a single mother."

I blinked. "Really? How did I not know that?"

Patrice gave me a wry smile. "I had to keep my own secrets and personal life for so long, it's hard for me to change that. But when I first started here as an associate professor, I was a single mom. Eventually, I got married and kept my last name because it was hard to explain to the boys of the department why I would want to change it." She rolled her eyes and I laughed.

"I can only imagine."

"My kids, all of them, added my name to my husband's. My husband's is even hyphenated. It was easier for everybody involved, even though their names went a little long. Now I'm about to be a grandmother, and I'm looking towards the future. Knowing that while there may be bumps in the road, women in science have a future because of people like you. So, one day when you're not rushing home to be with your baby, we should have a drink. I think my kids would love to meet you as well. My youngest daughter wants to be a physicist too, and it just makes me grin."

I nearly wanted to cry, knowing that this move out here had been the best choice for me. Landon had tried to take it from me, but in the end, he didn't matter. It was everybody left behind that did. Making the choice to come out here, to change everything, had been the best one.

I had this department, my team, and I was making a family.

I smiled to myself as I packed up my belongings and headed home, knowing that I had an early day tomorrow. Research was going well, but it still took hours of my life just to untangle the data. While some professors might just let their students take over, that wasn't me. I loved to be in the thick of it.

I pulled into the driveway, the garage door was closed, but I knew it was full of kitchen cabinets. Leif and some of his family had come over the day before to help me sand them down because we were going to paint them. They needed to be refinished, and since I was dating somebody who had family with an actual homebuilding business who knew what they were doing, I wanted to use my resources.

It was also nice that I could lean on someone, and ask for help, and know that there were talented individuals who would help, no matter what.

I got out of the car and waved at Lake, who pulled a hoodie over her head.

It was warm out, so I wondered why she was wearing a hoodie rather than her usual dressy outfit, but she just waved at me and then headed to her car without saying anything.

It was weird, but maybe she had places to go. I shook my head, headed inside, and grinned at the sight of Leif and Luke running around the house.

They were playing with some Nerf gun that Nick of all people had gotten them, and I laughed.

"Well, this is a sight to see."

"Mommy! Be on my team!" Luke said as he ran towards me. I threw my arms open and he jumped into them before I turned and blocked him from Leif's aim.

"I see how it is, two against one? I can take those odds."

"Where's May?" I asked.

"I finished with my client early, and Nick and the rest of the team had the shop covered, so I headed here. I let her go. That okay?" he asked, tentatively.

I grinned, my heart growing two sizes. "That's more than okay. She knows that you're allowed to be here anytime that you want, and you're also on my emergency contact list with the school. Everything's great, Leif."

It was the truth. Everything was great.

I was happy. My son was happy.

And I was in love with a man who loved me and my son.

Nothing could go wrong.

I put Luke down, picked up the spare Nerf gun, and winked.

"Okay, the battle is on."

Luke giggled, the laugh melting any ice that could have been lingering on my heart over any doubts I was doing the right thing, and then the battle was on.

In the end, Luke and I won, because of course we did. Leif made us a wonderful chicken piccata for dinner that made my mouth water, and we settled onto the couch to watch a kid show before bed. I snuggled into my son as Leif slid his arm over my shoulders.

"Love you," he whispered, and I grinned before leaning over Luke's head to kiss him gently.

"I like when you kiss," Luke said, and I looked down at him.

"You do?"

"It means you love each other. And I love you both." And then he settled back into the couch and focused on his TV show.

My throat tightened slightly, making it hard to swallow as Leif looked at me, his eyes watery.

That big man, with his beard, piercings, and tattoos, nearly crying over that, made my heart swell four sizes.

This was it. This was exactly what I wanted.

What exactly I thought I would never have after losing Luke's father all those years ago. He had never had a chance to meet Luke.

We had never had a chance to figure out how to co-parent without being in a relationship.

I missed him, in the sense that I missed the man he had been, but I had never loved that man.

But I loved who he gave me. Our son.

Now Leif was here. There was no going back.

Glass shattered behind us, and I threw myself over Luke as Leif did over both of us.

"Mommy?" Luke asked, and I scrambled off the couch, Luke in my arms.

"Quiet, baby," I whispered, holding him close.

Leif was in front of us, cursing under his breath.

"Roger. What are you doing here?"

I stood behind Leif, Luke in my arms, my eyes wide.

This was the man harassing Leif. This was the man who dated Leif's mother all those years ago. The man who had gone to prison and should still be there.

Apparently, the authorities hadn't convinced him to leave us alone.

And he knew where I lived. Where my son lived. My entire body was ice cold.

"I told you that I was going to find your girl and get what I wanted," the other man slurred.

He was drunk, that was for sure, and maybe on something else. Fear coated my tongue, and I held Luke tightly, hiding his face from this strange man. I didn't want my son to be scared, but it was hard for him not to be when I was terrified.

"I'm not sure what you want, but let's talk about it outside. You know this isn't the place to do this, Roger," Leif said, his voice oh so calm. But I heard the rage beneath his words. The fear. The same things that were within me.

"I want what I should've had. Your mom is the one that sent me to prison. Did you know that? She's the one that forced me to go. If she hadn't, I could've had this family. I could've had so much more. But now here you are, with Montgomery money, acting as if you're better than me? You're nothing." The other man tossed something at my lamp, shattering it.

That's when I realized he had a knife in one hand.

I looked down at the coffee table, where our phones were. I wanted to reach out, to call for help. Roger followed my gaze.

"You move towards that phone, and I stab this man

in front of me. This piece of trash. And then I'll come after you and that little boy. All I want is a few bucks to get me going. I have places to be. I've retribution coming to me. Places to be…"

"I can give you money, Roger. To get out of here, but if you stay here, the cops are going to come here. They're going to know you were here, and there's no going back from that. I'm sorry that my mother sent you to jail," Leif blatantly lied. "But we can't do anything for you here. I'm just a tattoo artist. I barely make rent."

Another lie.

"Brooke is a struggling single mom, we're trying, but we don't have the money that you want. None of my family does. We're blue-collar."

"You still think you're better than me."

"I'm sorry that you went to prison," I said, and Leif stiffened. He might not want me to speak, but I wasn't just going to stand by while we waited for Roger to do something. "I'm sorry," I repeated. "But coming here isn't going to help you. It can't. So why don't you leave, and we won't do anything."

"You're lying," he snarled, before he swayed.

Leif moved and I reached out, wanting to scream, but instead I held Luke back, shielding his eyes, trying to cover his ears.

Leif moved as if he had been born for this, as if he had fought strange, drunk men with knives all his life.

He took Roger's wrist, twisted as the man screamed.

When the knife dropped, I reached for the phone and quickly dialed 911.

Leif moved quickly, punching Roger in the face, and then knelt down over him, pinning his arms behind his back.

Roger was out, either drunk, or knocked out from the punch, and my knees shook as I listened to the 911 operator.

"Yes, ma'am, we received an alert from your security company, and people are on the way. Are you safe?"

I looked at Leif, at the way that he held Roger down, and at Luke as he held me tightly, but didn't cry, just trusted us to keep him safe.

"For now. Please hurry."

"Luke, you okay?" Leif asked, his eyes wide as he began to shake, even as he pinned Roger down.

I pushed Luke's hair back from his face and pressed my forehead to his.

"Are you okay, buddy?

"Of course, I am. I had you and Leif."

I nearly burst out crying, and only stopped because it would scare my son. I held myself back, clutching the phone, keeping Luke away from Roger. I wanted to hurt the man for daring to threaten my family, but I had to keep Luke safe.

Just like Leif had kept us safe.

"I love you," I gasped.

Leif gave me a small smile, even as guilt filled his gaze. "I love you, too."

"Don't blame yourself. This isn't your fault. It's his," I said, gesturing towards the unconscious man.

Leif's jaw tightened and he nodded as the sirens came. I let out a breath.

Things moved quickly then, the police entering my house, going through everything.

They checked over Luke, although he was perfectly fine according to the paramedics. I would take him to his pediatrician the next day, just in case. As well as find a child psychologist.

We stood in the front lawn, as the neighbors came outside to see what was going on, and Leif held me close, waiting.

"I love you," he whispered.

"I love you too. You better not blame yourself for this."

We were whispering now as Luke was passed out on my shoulder, sleeping hard after the adrenaline rush.

Leif moved, taking Luke in his arms, doing his best not to jostle him. I was grateful that I didn't have to carry my son for much longer since my arm was asleep, and I wrapped myself around them both, needing their touch.

"Roger's going away for a long time," I said, my voice low. "He came here because he had nowhere else to go, not because it's your fault. This is on him. Just like I don't get to blame myself for Landon's actions. You don't get to blame yourself for Roger's."

"I'm not quite sure I like you throwing my words back at me," he whispered before he kissed the top of my head. "I love you. I don't blame myself. But I am so fucking angry." He looked over my head and let out a soft laugh.

The fact that he was laughing at all told me that we were at least going in the right direction.

"The cavalry is here. Be prepared. The Montgomerys are on their way."

I turned and saw countless people that I knew, some that I didn't, but they all looked so much like Leif that I knew they had to be related.

The Montgomerys were coming in full force.

Family was coming in full force.

As the authorities let Leif's family come past the roped-off area, I let them hold me.

For once, I knew I would never be alone.

This wasn't just Luke and me facing the world.

I had a man that I loved. The family we were making. An extended family that was far larger than I had ever once thought possible.

I had fallen for a Montgomery. That meant I would face the future with them, too.

I made a promise to myself when I was younger, that I would try to fight the darkness and face the world even if I was on my own.

But now, I would get to break that promise because I would never be alone.

I would never have to be.

Chapter 20

Leif

I had made a promise while on the Eiffel Tower, like any young man who fell in love and lust with a young woman that he couldn't have.

The fact that we had broken our promises left a bittersweet taste on my tongue, but in the end, we had grown into the people that we needed to be.

I was Leif Montgomery, son, brother, cousin, friend, and, one day husband and father.

All of those words wrapped up into an enigma of who I was, a complicated man who was trying to find his way. At least, that's what Brooke told me. And I always listen to what she said, with a yes ma'am, a gleam in my eye, and a kiss on her lips.

"Are you ready for this?" I asked as I looked over at Brooke, with Luke standing between us, holding each of our hands.

"It's not going to be that bad," she said and I laughed. Luke joined me, and then the door opened, the noise chaotic and brilliant.

It was my mother's birthday, and while it would've been fun to get all of the family together, not everybody could make it. They had decided to hold the festivities with just the family in this part of the branch rather than everyone in the area. It got a little insane if you went past those numbers and we wouldn't fit in the house.

"You're here!" Colin grinned, and my brother came forward and picked Luke up. He spun the kid around and then ran into the house with him, leaving us behind.

Brooke blinked. "Well, nice to see you, too, Colin."

"Look how I feel. I'm related to the kid," I said with a laugh, before I gripped my mother's present firmly in one hand, took Brooke's hand with my other, and made my way inside.

My aunts and uncles and most of their teenage and adult children were in the house, laughing, talking about cheese boards, presents, and an upcoming football game.

My dad stood near the front window, laughing at something my uncle Alex said. Sebastian stood between them, weariness in his gaze. I knew he told his parents and other members of the family about the pregnancy. I didn't know what would happen next or how he would handle it, but he would. Because my cousin was intelligent, responsible, and strong, and so was his girlfriend. They would figure it out.

And we would be there if they needed us.

"There you are," my dad said as he came forward, a smile on his face. "We were afraid you got lost."

"That was my fault," Brooke said as she hugged my dad back. "I had a last-minute meeting with one of my students. She has her huge presentation next week and had a slight panic attack."

Austin nodded, his eyes full of understanding. "I know how that feels. Not that I went to college or grad school, but presentations were never my thing."

"I find that hilarious considering all you do is talk and tell us what to do," Uncle Alex said with a wink.

Even as my dad scowled, I laughed, and Brooke wrapped her arm around my waist.

In the week since the attack and break-in, we had been dealing. Trying to figure out our path and how to heal. We stayed at my house more than hers because of the cleanup and memories. But we had yet to spend the night apart, and Luke was okay with it, and we were finding our routine.

Soon we would have to decide where to live, because I wasn't letting my new family out of my sight.

My lips twisted into a grin at the word family, and Brooke gave me a look.

"What?" she asked.

"Just thinking that I love you."

"Well, isn't that nauseating," Noah, another one of my cousins, said as he came up and hugged Brooke. "I can't believe he found you first. I'm sad."

Brooke snorted. "I'm nearly a decade older than you, darling. I don't think you could handle this."

Everybody whistled, and Noah just took it in stride. "Oh, I'm going to have fun finding a woman like you when my time comes. I'm going to take my time though. I'm not like Sebastian here, jumping the gun."

Sebastian flipped him off as everyone laughed. "I can't help it. I found the love of my life early."

I looked down at Brooke. "So did I. It just took me a little bit longer to find her again."

Brooke blushed and my dad cleared his throat. "Is that a present for your mom? We have the table over there. That way, you don't have to hold it this whole time."

"I want to hand this to her. Is that okay?" I asked.

"You don't have to ask me, son." My dad squeezed my shoulder and went back into conversation with the others. I took Brooke's hand and led her towards the back, where my mother held court with a few of my aunts. Aunt Maya grinned at me and waved at Brooke before I leaned down and kissed the top of my mom's head.

"Happy birthday, Mom."

"We're not going to mention what year it is. While I am grateful for growing into this age of not giving a fuck, I don't need the number."

I chuckled as Brooke and my mother fist-bumped.

"That sounds like a plan. Here you go. I wanted to give this to you rather than wait for you to open it later." I knew nerves were apparent in my voice. Brooke squeezed my hand.

My mom seemed to sense it because she quickly set down her drink and opened up the bag.

Maya leaned forward, wanting a look, and my mom waved her off, laughing.

"Oh, Leif," she whispered, opening the sketchbook.

"I have been working on it for the past couple of years, not quite sure what I would do with it when I was done. You can work out a few pages if you want to frame them, throw them away, or do whatever you want. But I don't know, it just felt right."

Tears were streaming down my mother's face as she turned the pages of the hand-drawn sketches I had made over the past year. Sketches of my parents, my brothers, sister, Brooke, and Luke. Nick laughing, Lake going over the books with that brilliant smile of hers.

Sebastian and Marley dancing. It was the people in my life who had brought me here.

I was a tattooist, an artist, son, brother, cousin—all of those labels I had been given before, and they were all encompassed in that sketchbook.

My mom stood up and cupped my face. I leaned down so she could kiss my cheek. "You are a brilliant, wonderful, talented man. Thank you for letting me be your mother."

I swallowed the hard lump in my throat. "Thank you for being my mother. Thank you for taking me in."

Others around us were sniffling now as Mom held me close. "I love you, Montgomery. All of you."

"And that's it for me," Brooke said as she pulled a tissue out of her purse, handing one to Maya before wiping her face.

"You're stuck with us now, girl," Maya said with a laugh, and she held Brooke close.

As I looked over my mother's head at Brooke, at how my family had taken to her, as I heard Luke's laughter in the back, I knew that these were the promises I had made. The promises I would keep.

I was a Montgomery. And that pretty much said everything.

Chapter 21

Lake

"WHAT IS THE POINT OF SPENDING ALL THIS MONEY ON concealers when they don't work?" My voice shook as I stood in front of the mirror, my hands unsteady. I had fourteen tubes, pots, and other containers of concealers strewn about on my counter.

Zach would hate the mess. He would tell me to clean it up. And then he would force me to clean it over and over again until it was exactly how he wanted.

And I would do it. Because I wanted to make him happy.

I looked at the different shades of pink, cream, and

beige on my counter and gripped the edge of the marble, trying to suck in a breath.

Everything hurt. How could this have happened?

This was on me.

I wasn't someone who got hurt like this. I was smarter than this. It was my fault, because I hadn't seen the signs even though I worked with people who did it daily.

It was my fault that I had allowed this to happen.

I was going to fix it because it wouldn't happen again.

I picked up the final tube of concealer in hopes that this one would work. That it would be the correct shade to cover up the bruising.

Tears bit at my eyes. My lip ached from the cut in its flesh.

I could see his hand marks on my neck. The width of his fingers with every achingly slow squeeze of his hand as he looked at me and told me I was nothing.

I could trace his thumb along my throat, his fingertip brushing my chin.

I could see the edge of the bruising already forming after such a short time on my neck, down to my shoulders. I could see where he had tried to choke me, to end me because I had said no.

My lip still had a cut that had finally stopped bleed-ing, and the bruise around my eye would eventually fade. The concealer did a better job of hiding that, but not as good a job as I needed it to.

I needed to hide it so the others couldn't see. So I could fix this on my own.

I was Lake Montgomery. I had been pulled out of my own hell once before and been blessed into this family. I couldn't shame them by telling them I had made a mistake. A mistake that would cost me everything.

I could not cry, I could not weep, I could not break. Because none of that would help. Nothing could help. But all the money spent on concealers in the world was not going to hide these bruises.

Nothing would hide these bruises.

With a cry, I shoved the concealers into the sink, the act of violence causing bile to rise in my throat. I needed to breathe, needing to do anything but stand here and feel sorry for myself.

Other people had it much worse than I did. They were living paycheck to paycheck, living out of their cars, needing help when I didn't. I helped others.

I didn't *need* help.

I pressed my hand to my side, the sharp pain making it harder to breathe.

I met my gaze in the mirror, the blue faded.

When had that happened? When had my eyes changed color?

I swallowed hard, my throat dry. It hurt to think, it hurt to breathe.

If I didn't need help, why was I putting concealer on my neck at seven p.m.?

If no one was going to see me, why was I trying to hide it?

I stood there, my thoughts going in a chaotic swirl as I tried to remember everything that happened and what I needed to do. I needed to leave, to stay away. I needed to hide. I needed to run. I need to do anything but stand here and wonder why I didn't have the perfect shade of pink concealer to cover up Zach's handprints on my neck.

"I need help," I whispered, the words broken, shattered remnants of the person I had been.

I was Lake Montgomery. A millionaire who was brilliant in tech and could form a business that helped others. Who *constantly* helped others.

I was not the woman in the mirror. The shadowed reflection of a wraith.

I closed my eyes, trying to find a semblance of composure. But there was nothing.

My phone was broken, my purse long gone. He had taken everything.

He had taken me.

I stumbled out of the bathroom, through my bedroom, and down the hallway. I moved past the broken lamp, the upturned chair. I kept walking over the glass shards, ignoring the searing pain in my feet. Then I opened the door and kept moving. I just kept moving.

Although Leif and Brooke would be moving soon, I knew they would be over there. Because Luke still lived there. *That little boy.*

I hoped it was late enough that he was sleeping because I didn't want him to see me. I didn't want anyone to see me.

I needed something. I just couldn't remember what it was. My head hurt, and I felt as if I saw double every other time I blinked. Things weren't making sense, and I had a hard time keeping my thoughts in order.

I moved across the grass achingly slow, ignoring the piercing shards of pain in my feet and down my sides.

I just needed Leif. My cousin would help.

He always helped. He wouldn't hate me. I didn't want him to hate me.

I moved up the porch, sucking in a breath as I tried to move one foot in front of another. I wanted to sleep. If I slept, things would be better. I would be able to breathe, and nothing would hurt anymore.

I needed my cousin. He would know what to do.

The door swung open before I could knock, and I saw the one person I didn't want to see. I would rather see anyone other than him.

No, that was a lie. I didn't want to see my parents, not now. They couldn't see this.

And I couldn't see Zach.

It became harder and harder to breathe. I knew I was hyperventilating. I had to be stronger than this.

I *was* stronger than this.

"Lake? What the hell, baby?" His voice was so soft. So unlike the Nick I knew. Maybe this wasn't him? Maybe it was Zach pretending to be him. Alarm shot through me. I needed to run.

And then Nick was there, coming closer. I cringed instinctively, my body stiffening.

I saw the storm echo over his face before he cooled his features, looking as if he hadn't wanted to break down the walls around us, to tear through anything between us.

This was Nick. My cousin's best friend, my family's friend.

My friend. A business partner.

My jokingly fake nemesis.

And I didn't want him to see me like this.

"Lake. Baby. What happened?"

"Nick?" I croaked, my voice hurt. Everything hurt.

Why was he here? I thought that Leif would be here, not Nick. Nick didn't live here. I knew that. Why was I telling myself these things that were true and yet not relevant? Why was everything taking so long to think through?

I wanted to hide. I wanted to go away. I wanted to

pretend this never happened. But I had been doing that for far too long. I had nowhere else to go.

So I said the one thing I didn't want to, but the only thing that I knew would change everything. Because this was next, if my cousin wasn't here, then Nick would be there. Because he always was. *Always.*

"I need help."

My knees gave out and Nick caught me, saying words I didn't understand. I knew that everything would be okay because Nick was here.

Even if nothing was ever okay again.

***

NEXT IN THE MONTGOMERY INK LEGACY SERIES:
Lake and Nick take a chance in AT FIRST MEET.

If you'd like to read a bonus scene from LEIF & BROOKE:
Check out this special Epilogue!

A Note from Carrie Ann Ryan

Thank you so much for reading **BITTERSWEET PROMISES.**

Going back to the origins of the Montgomerys was like going back in time and yet flinging myself into the future all at once.

When Leif first strolled onto the series into the first book, he was an adorable 10 year old kid. Over the past decade, I've watched him grow into an adult on page and now being able to write his romance was something I'll always cherish.

He's the man I knew I needed to write, the story I knew that wasn't finished. And he's only the beginning with this series.

Brooke?

Brooke is my heart mate. I adore her and am

blessed to have been able to write her story. (And Luke? Well…that kid has my heart.)

I cannot wait to dive deep into the next generation of the Montgomerys. Because no matter what, if you're a longtime fan of this series, these stories will be for you. And if this is the first book you've read from me, this is the best place to start. Because it's all new.

It's just for you.

And we're just getting started.

Lake and Nick are next and their book has already broke my heart. I cannot wait for their story!

The Montgomery Ink Legacy Series:

Book 1: Bittersweet Promises

Book 2: At First Meet

Book 2.5: Happily Ever Never

Book 3: Longtime Crush

IF YOU'D LIKE TO READ A BONUS SCENE FROM **LEIF & BROOKE:**
CHECK OUT THIS SPECIAL EPILOGUE!

NEXT IN THE MONTGOMERY INK LEGACY SERIES:
Lake and Nick take a chance in AT FIRST MEET.

If you want to make sure you know what's coming next

from me, you can sign up for my newsletter at www.
CarrieAnnRyan.com; follow me on twitter at
@CarrieAnnRyan, or like my Facebook page. I also
have a Facebook Fan Club where we have trivia, chats,
and other goodies. You guys are the reason I get to do
what I do and I thank you.

Make sure you're signed up for my MAILING LIST so
you can know when the next releases are available as
well as find giveaways and FREE READS.

Happy Reading!

Also from Carrie Ann Ryan

The Montgomery Ink Legacy Series:
Book 1: Bittersweet Promises
Book 2: At First Meet
Book 2.5: Happily Ever Never
Book 3: Longtime Crush

The Wilder Brothers Series:
Book 1: One Way Back to Me
Book 2: Always the One for Me
Book 3: The Path to You
Book 4: Coming Home for Us

The Aspen Pack Series:
Book 1: Etched in Honor
Book 2: Hunted in Darkness
Book 3: Mated in Chaos

Book 4: Harbored in Silence

The Montgomery Ink: Fort Collins Series:
Book 1: Inked Persuasion

Book 2: Inked Obsession

Book 3: Inked Devotion

Book 3.5: Nothing But Ink

Book 4: Inked Craving

Book 5: Inked Temptation

The Montgomery Ink: Boulder Series:
Book 1: Wrapped in Ink

Book 2: Sated in Ink

Book 3: Embraced in Ink

Book 3: Moments in Ink

Book 4: Seduced in Ink

Book 4.5: Captured in Ink

Book 4.7: Inked Fantasy

Book 4.8: A Very Montgomery Christmas

Montgomery Ink: Colorado Springs
Book 1: Fallen Ink

Book 2: Restless Ink

Book 2.5: Ashes to Ink

Book 3: Jagged Ink

Book 3.5: Ink by Numbers

Montgomery Ink Denver:

Book 0.5: Ink Inspired
Book 0.6: Ink Reunited
Book 1: Delicate Ink
Book 1.5: Forever Ink
Book 2: Tempting Boundaries
Book 3: Harder than Words
Book 3.5: Finally Found You
Book 4: Written in Ink
Book 4.5: Hidden Ink
Book 5: Ink Enduring
Book 6: Ink Exposed
Book 6.5: Adoring Ink
Book 6.6: Love, Honor, & Ink
Book 7: Inked Expressions
Book 7.3: Dropout
Book 7.5: Executive Ink
Book 8: Inked Memories
Book 8.5: Inked Nights
Book 8.7: Second Chance Ink
Book 8.5: Montgomery Midnight Kisses
Bonus: Inked Kingdom

The On My Own Series:
Book 0.5: My First Glance
Book 1: My One Night
Book 2: My Rebound
Book 3: My Next Play
Book 4: My Bad Decisions

The Promise Me Series:
Book 1: Forever Only Once
Book 2: From That Moment
Book 3: Far From Destined
Book 4: From Our First

The Less Than Series:
Book 1: Breathless With Her
Book 2: Reckless With You
Book 3: Shameless With Him

The Fractured Connections Series:
Book 1: Breaking Without You
Book 2: Shouldn't Have You
Book 3: Falling With You
Book 4: Taken With You

The Whiskey and Lies Series:
Book 1: Whiskey Secrets
Book 2: Whiskey Reveals
Book 3: Whiskey Undone

The Gallagher Brothers Series:
Book 1: Love Restored
Book 2: Passion Restored
Book 3: Hope Restored

The Ravenwood Coven Series:

Book 1: Dawn Unearthed

Book 2: Dusk Unveiled

Book 3: Evernight Unleashed

The Talon Pack:

Book 1: Tattered Loyalties

Book 2: An Alpha's Choice

Book 3: Mated in Mist

Book 4: Wolf Betrayed

Book 5: Fractured Silence

Book 6: Destiny Disgraced

Book 7: Eternal Mourning

Book 8: Strength Enduring

Book 9: Forever Broken

Book 10: Mated in Darkness

Book 11: Fated in Winter

Redwood Pack Series:

Book 1: An Alpha's Path

Book 2: A Taste for a Mate

Book 3: Trinity Bound

Book 3.5: A Night Away

Book 4: Enforcer's Redemption

Book 4.5: Blurred Expectations

Book 4.7: Forgiveness

Book 5: Shattered Emotions

Book 6: Hidden Destiny

Book 6.5: A Beta's Haven

Book 7: Fighting Fate

Book 7.5: Loving the Omega

Book 7.7: The Hunted Heart

Book 8: Wicked Wolf

The Elements of Five Series:

Book 1: From Breath and Ruin

Book 2: From Flame and Ash

Book 3: From Spirit and Binding

Book 4: From Shadow and Silence

Dante's Circle Series:

Book 1: Dust of My Wings

Book 2: Her Warriors' Three Wishes

Book 3: An Unlucky Moon

Book 3.5: His Choice

Book 4: Tangled Innocence

Book 5: Fierce Enchantment

Book 6: An Immortal's Song

Book 7: Prowled Darkness

Book 8: Dante's Circle Reborn

Holiday, Montana Series:

Book 1: Charmed Spirits

Book 2: Santa's Executive

Book 3: Finding Abigail

Book 4: Her Lucky Love

Book 5: Dreams of Ivory

The Branded Pack Series:
(Written with Alexandra Ivy)

Book 1: Stolen and Forgiven

Book 2: Abandoned and Unseen

Book 3: Buried and Shadowed

About the Author

Carrie Ann Ryan is the New York Times and USA Today bestselling author of contemporary, paranormal, and young adult romance. Her works include the Montgomery Ink, Redwood Pack, Fractured Connections, and Elements of Five series, which have sold over 3.0 million books worldwide. She started writing while in graduate school for her advanced degree in chemistry and hasn't stopped since. Carrie Ann has written over seventy-five novels and novellas with more in the works. When she's not losing herself in her emotional and action-packed worlds, she's reading as much as she can while wrangling her clowder of cats who have more followers than she does.

www.CarrieAnnRyan.com